Through
the
Storm

Eyum Ejiga
Author: "He Gave Me Comfort"

Impact Life Publisher
www.mypainyourgainminstries.com
Email: info@mypainyourgainministries.com

ISBN: 978-0-9574241-4-2

"After every storm the sun will smile;
For every problem there is a solution,
And the soul's indefeasible duty is to be of
good cheer."

- William R. Alger

Prologue

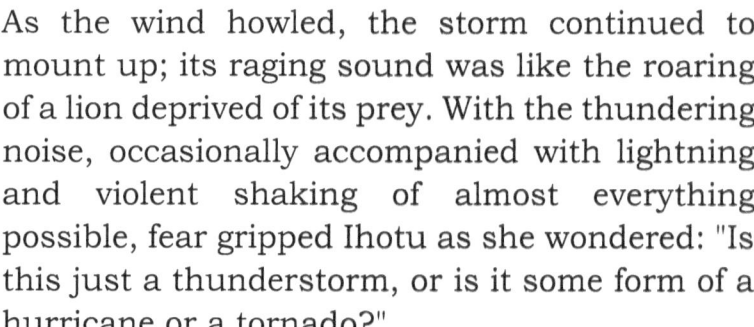

As the wind howled, the storm continued to mount up; its raging sound was like the roaring of a lion deprived of its prey. With the thundering noise, occasionally accompanied with lightning and violent shaking of almost everything possible, fear gripped Ihotu as she wondered: "Is this just a thunderstorm, or is it some form of a hurricane or a tornado?"

It could sometimes be quite windy in Ireland, but she had never experienced this kind of storm. As she looked out of her window, she saw that motorists were parking their cars by the roadside as the wind could almost throw any moving vehicle off the road. She could see that some loose roof tiles had been blown away and some trees were already knocked down.

As the storm continued, she couldn't help but compare it to the numerous shakings she had experienced in her life. Tears, tears, and much tears had filled most of her life from a very early age up to her early adulthood. "Just when I thought things were beginning to settle down for me, another storm hits again! Will the storms never cease in my life?" Ihotu had often wondered. The storms of life usually come upon us suddenly and they can be very violent, turbulent as well as unpredictable.

Now at the age of twenty-four, Ihotu is looking back and can hardly believe that she actually made it through her own personal storm. With her wedding just a few months away and with the excellent job she is now enjoying, many people have looked at her and exclaimed, "How lucky she is." The last time she visited her home country, she even overheard some folks saying that they wished they were her. "If only they knew what I have passed through, they would never wish to be me." She would typically smile and say this to herself when she heard such comments. Very few people know the story behind this seeming success of her life. She is certain that not many people of her age would have endured the pains that she had suffered to get to where she is today.

As her thoughts alternated between this on-going storm and her life's experiences, the thunder struck loudly again, and she momentarily looked for a solid support to hold on to with the fear that their house was probably going to collapse. She wondered whether this storm could be comparable to hurricanes like Alice, Katrina or Sandy that she had heard about. "By the way, why are these deadly storms mostly given cute female names?" she asked herself and this brought a smile to her face, as she began to reminisce about the different experiences she had gone through in her journey of life.

Chapter 1

Edache Edeh, a younger brother of Ihotu's mum had brought Ihotu to live with him and his family in Dublin when she was ten years old. Ihotu is the eldest of her mum's three children and they had lost their dad in a ghastly motor accident just two years previously. Life was quite comfortable for them before the untimely death of her father as he had been a successful businessman. It was on one of his business trips that death came suddenly and snatched his life away.

Mr. Ameh, Ihotu's dad had lived in Victoria Island (popularly called VI), Lagos with his wife, Ahubi, and their two children, Ihotu and Agada, before his sudden death on that fateful Monday morning. Victoria Island is an exclusive and expensive part of Lagos that is occupied by mostly the rich and affluent in society. Mr. Ameh was a successful importer of telephone handsets and accessories and, with the accessibility and increasing use of mobile phones by almost everyone in Nigeria, his business was doing very well. A few years beforehand, only the rich people used mobile phones but now, even a fruit-seller by the roadside owned one, and so his business had great prospects. It was on one of his trips to the seaport that morning, to clear a container of goods that had arrived for him at the Lagos port when the accident happened. His wife, Ahubi was thirty-six weeks pregnant when the news of her husband's death reached her. This made her go into premature labour and she gave birth to their third child, a baby girl.

Due to the circumstances surrounding this child's birth, Ahubi's mother named her *Ikwubiela* meaning 'death has ruined things', but Ahubi being a Christian and understanding the power of names called her Precious. She reasoned that her baby was not the cause of her husband's death and so she did not want her to have a name that would constantly remind them of the incident. Neither did she want her child to have a name whose meaning could hurt her in the future as she believed that people lived out the meaning of their names. However, with her husband's corpse lying there in the mortuary, she did not have the strength to explain to her mum why didn't want her baby named Ikwubiela. She just quietly told her that she would prefer her to be called Precious. Her mum had meant well for Ahubi and her new-born baby and understood that this was not the time to argue about names. She had done what she knew how to do in the best possible way that she could. In her day, a child was named either after a favourite family member or based on an incident that happened during the birth of that child.

Things were never the same again in the family that Mr. Ameh left behind. Death is really cruel, and it ruined everything for Ahubi and her three children. Ahubi, who had obtained a combined honours degree in Chemistry and Education from the University of Jos, ten years before this incident, had never really been in paid employment all her life. The only work experience she had was as a teacher in a private secondary school in Lagos where she had done her National Youth Service.

The National Youth Service Corps (NYSC) is a compulsory service scheme instituted by the government of Nigeria to provide work experience for young University and Polytechnic graduates and to also involve them in the development of the nation. Under this scheme, every graduate is expected to serve the nation for one year but, by age, certain people can apply to be exempted. The participants are usually posted to other parts of the country that are far from the schools that they finished from and different from their states of origin. For instance, a graduate from northern Nigeria, who also schooled in the north is usually posted to serve in the eastern or southern parts, while it is the other way round for those coming from the east or the south. The aim of this is to encourage ethnic, social and cultural integration hence strengthening the unity of the country since Nigeria is such a huge country in terms of its land-size, population, tribal languages, and cultures. It was during this NYSC scheme that Mr. Ameh met the tall and ebony-skinned Ahubi and they got married immediately after the end of the programme.

Mr. Ameh, who was in his mid-thirties at the time, was already under pressure from his parents to 'settle down'. He understood clearly that 'settling down' meant marrying a wife and having children, but while many of the young ladies that he had met in Lagos were good-looking, they all lacked the good character he wanted for his wife to have. He did not buy into his father's idea when he suggested that they look for a young girl of good character from their village for him to marry. This was why, when he saw the combination of beauty and good character in Ahubi, he couldn't wait to marry her.

Ahubi and her husband started a family immediately and, because they were financially comfortable, Mr. Ameh persuaded her not to take up a job so that she could have the time to take care of their young family. He promised to set up a business for her after their third baby was born and was old enough to be weaned, as that would be their last child. Unfortunately, Mr. Ameh did not live to see his third child born.

As Mr. Ameh's telecommunications business was booming at the time, he had taken a loan of a substantial sum of money to expand the business. He had used their family house at VI as collateral for the loan as he was very optimistic that he would pay off the loan in no time because of the attractive profit margins in the business. However, all his carefully laid out plans came crashing down on that fateful morning of his death. Man, they say, proposes but God disposes!

Things turned for the worse for Ahubi and her children soon after the burial of Mr. Ameh. The bank came demanding their money back and, because there was no other way to pay it, they re-possessed his house and the container of goods that he had just imported before his death. Apart from this family house in Lagos, the only other property Mr. Ameh had owned, was a three-bedroom bungalow in Otukpo, his home town. As Ahubi and her children had to leave their home following the repossession by the bank, she had no choice but to move with them into the house in Otukpo even though it was not in the best habitable state. Mr. Ameh had purchased this dilapidated house about a year before that time, with the intention of renovating it before December of that year as the entire family was planning to spend Christmas at home. He also planned that this house would serve as a holiday home for him and his family whenever they visited Otukpo, as previously they usually had stayed in hotels any time they were visiting.

Life indeed is like a flower that can be flourishing in the morning but withered by evening time. Who would have thought that Ahubi and her children, who had been enjoying so much comfort and luxury just a few months before, would now find themselves reduced to living in such a low state? Soon after moving, Ahubi found a job in a private secondary school owned by her uncle and was given the opportunity to teach chemistry. However, the salary was quite meagre, it was barely enough to feed herself and her children let alone provide for their other needs. Meeting basic needs such as clothing and school fees for her children soon became an ordeal. It was amid these difficulties that Edache, Ahubi's younger brother who had migrated to the Republic of Ireland a few years before that time, showed up and offered to take Ihotu to Ireland and to bring her up as his own child. Even though it was very difficult for Ahubi to part with Ihotu, the prospect of her having a better life with better educational opportunities in Ireland, which should translate into a chance for a better future for her daughter, made her reluctantly accept Edache's offer.

"Edache, my children are all that I have left in this life," Ahubi said in the midst of tears as she handed Ihotu over to her brother. "Please take good care of her and treat her as your child. Love and discipline her as you would any of your own children."

Before their departure, as she hugged Ihotu, she said to her, "*Ihotu kum*' (which means 'my Love'), you know how dear you are to me. I wish I didn't have to make this decision, but because I believe your future will be better if I let you go to Ireland with your uncle, this is why I am letting go of you. You know the daughter of whom you are. Please keep up your good behaviour and may God always be with you." As both mother and child hugged each other and wept uncontrollably, Ihotu's little brother and sister joined in, and the whole family pledged their love for her before she left with her uncle.

Chapter 2

As the plane came in to land, Ihotu was overwhelmed with joy. She couldn't believe that this was her, coming not to visit but to live in the white man's land. The only trip she had ever made outside of her home country before now was to Dubai when her dad had taken the whole family there for a Christmas holiday when she was six years old. Although that trip had been only about four years before now, the hardship of the last two years following his death seemed to have completely wiped out the memory of it. Her dad had been planning to take them to London in August for the summer holidays and had even obtained visas for the trip, but then came the awful event of his death that year.

Ihotu kept asking her uncle, Edache, question after question right from the time they arrived at Murtala Mohammed International Airport in Lagos where they were to board their flight with Air France. Even on board the plane, her questions continued ceaselessly but Edache, understanding her excitement, didn't tire of answering her. She eventually fell asleep about two hours into the flight when it was a little past midnight because it was a night flight.

The slight bump of the plane landing awakened Ihotu from her sleep, and she excitedly asked:

"Uncle, are we in Ireland now?"

She was a little disappointed when her uncle told her that they had just arrived in Paris and would be continuing their journey to Dublin after another two hours.

"Oh, this Dublin is too far," she exclaimed! "Why did the plane bring us to Paris instead of Dublin?"

Edache then took time to explain to her that they were transiting in Paris because there were no direct flights from Lagos to Dublin. He told her that Paris was not too far away from Ireland and that, once they took off, they would be there after a very short time.

The two hours they had to wait in Paris seemed like two days to Ihotu. However, Charles de Gaulle Airport was a lovely place, and it was fascinating for Ihotu to see so many white people. She laughed to herself when she thought of how her uncle, herself and the few other black people around, stood out among the crowds of white people. In Nigeria, the reverse would have been the case, and a white person would always stand out because he is in the midst of so many black people. Her uncle walked her around the airport to see the various beautiful sights and, after a while, they settled into some vacant seats to wait for their flight.

When Edache finally announced to her that it was time for them to board their flight to Dublin, Ihotu could not contain her joy. She constantly walked ahead of him, and he had to keep calling her back so that she would not lose her way out of excitement. On the flight, Ihotu hardly ate anything as she felt too happy to be hungry and even more so because most of the food that was served was strange to her.

When their plane finally touched down in Dublin, Edache announced to her, "Ihotu, we are in Ireland!" Small tears of joy dropped from her eyes as she said a quiet prayer to God for bringing her safely to Dublin. It still seemed like a dream to her even though she knew she wasn't dreaming. After passing through Immigration and collecting their luggage, they walked out into the Arrivals Hall, and there were Edache's wife, Ebere, and their two children who were waiting to welcome them.

They had been waiting for about forty-five minutes before Edache and Ihotu arrived. As their children, Ene and Ehi had been told so many things about their big cousin, they excitedly hugged and welcomed her as their dad introduced her to them. Ebere was pleased to have Ihotu stay with them as she hoped that Ihotu would help her with the housework. Her children were too young to be of much help, but instead, they needed a lot of help themselves.

As they stepped out of the Arrivals Hall to proceed to the car park, a cool Irish summer breeze embraced them and Ihotu began to shiver.

"Don't tell me you are cold! I'm roasting!" Ene blurted out.

Even though this was a bright summer morning with the sun shining and the temperature about twenty degrees Celsius, it felt cold for this young Nigerian girl who was coming from a place where the average temperature would be about thirty-four degrees Celsius. As soon as they got into the car, the first thing Ihotu noticed was that the steering wheel was on the right-hand side instead of on the left as was the case in Nigeria. As the heater warmed up the car, Ihotu began to feel more comfortable, and her questions started again.

"Uncle, what is wrong with this car? Why is the steering on the right and not on the left? And why are we also driving on the wrong side of the road?" Ihotu asked.

Edache explained to her that nothing was wrong with the car and neither were they driving on the wrong side of the road. He explained to her that as one travels around the world, one sees that the same things can be done in different ways and so the steering on the right and the driving on the left are normal things in Ireland. He then went on to inform the family that because Ihotu was coming to Ireland for the first time, a lot of things would look strange to her and that they would need to be patient with her. As Ihotu settled back into her little corner of the car to take in a bit of Ireland as she looked out of the window, it was now the turn of Ene and Ehi to start asking her their questions.

"Ihotu, is it true that little kids starve in Africa?" Ehi asked. "Mum always tells me not to waste food because little kids are starving in Africa."

Ihotu found it a bit difficult to understand Ehi and Ene when they spoke because of their Irish accent. As she was trying to fully figure out what Ehi was saying, Edache came to her rescue by asking them, "Does Ihotu look starved?"

"Nope," Ene admitted as she joined in the conversation. She could see that Ihotu was a slender lively girl. Even though she was very slim, she still looked fresh, and her complexion was a bit lighter than chocolate. This was because her mum had always ensured that they ate balanced diets. So, even when she couldn't afford meat in their meals, she had substituted their source of protein and iron with things like beans and vegetables. She had also made milk from soya beans.

"We are always asked to donate money at school to send to hungry kids in Africa as well," Ene added.

"And charity bags are always being dropped at our house, asking for donations of clothing and other materials to be sent to needy children in Africa, aren't they?" Edache asked.

"Yeah!" Ene and Ehi agreed simultaneously.

Their dad went on to explain that there are starving children and people in need in many parts of the world, but that Africa seems to have a large percentage of them because it is still a developing continent. He said that the images of Africa shown by people soliciting for these donations were sometimes exaggerated to whip up sentiment so that people would be moved to donate more generously. He finished by saying, "As you can see, Ihotu doesn't look like she is starved, so not all kids in Africa are starving."

As they made their way through Dublin City, Ihotu couldn't help comparing Ireland with Nigeria, from where she had just come. Ireland looked beautiful, and the road network with all the different road signs seemed great, but having visited Abuja, the capital city of Nigeria before, she concluded that Dublin was just as beautiful. Ebere, who had been silent while driving all the while pulled over and stopped at the front of a house, Ihotu's thoughts were momentarily interrupted when her uncle announced to her that they had arrived home.

The house was beautiful and looked quite new. It was a three-bedroom semi-detached house that Edache and Ebere had purchased on mortgage about two years earlier. The garden at the front of the house looked well-kept and had some nice flowers growing in them. As they stepped into the sitting room, Ebere ordered her children to pick up their toys that they had left littered all over the place from the previous night and hadn't had the time to tidy up that morning before they left hastily for the airport.

The living room was tastefully furnished with a gorgeous set of leather sofas, big plasma television and other state-of-the-art gadgets. However, Ihotu found the room quite small as the furniture and gadgets were all tightly arranged with very little space left for moving around. As she looked from one place to another, she remembered the gigantic living rooms that the rich people in Nigeria had. She particularly remembered her paternal uncle's house in Abuja where there were three huge sitting-rooms. When she visited that uncle of hers with her mum a year earlier, she had asked them why they had so many sitting-rooms. She was told that one was for the children, the next was for the parents, and the third was the executive sitting-room where her uncle received his business colleagues and people very special to him. This last one was hardly ever used because his business colleagues were mostly received in his office.

When Ihotu was taken upstairs and shown her bed-room, she felt disappointed at the size of it. Apart from the small six-inch bed and the slimly fitted wardrobe, there was no space for any further furniture in the room. Her room in her under-developed little town of Otukpo was about three times the size of this one! This room being given to her used to be Ehi's room, and Ehi had moved into Ene's room to share it with her to create space for Ihotu. Their room wasn't too big either. It was fitted with a bunk bed and was probably about one and a half times the size of the room that was to be hers. The only reasonably spacious room was Edache and Ebere's bed-room, and it had a bathroom en-suite. People in the other two rooms had to share a toilet and a bathroom which was located just next to the smaller room. Ihotu felt disappointed as she thought to herself, "Is this Europe? I thought the rooms in Europe would look like the mansions we are told about in the Bible that are being prepared in heaven for us!" Later, when she asked her uncle why all the rooms were so tiny compared to the rooms in Nigeria, he told her that moderation was the order of the day here in Europe as there was little or no room for waste. A bigger house would mean more bills to pay as the cost of heating, cleaning and maintenance would also increase.

****

As August gave way to September, the time came for the new school year to begin. Ihotu was ten years old and would be eleven in November. In

Ireland, the school system is such that children normally start primary school at the age of six but must turn six before September of that school year. Any child whose sixth birthday falls in September or the months after must wait until the following year to be enrolled. This meant that Ihotu would have to go into fourth class instead of fifth which she could have joined had she been born before September. She was not happy about this because, before she left Nigeria, she had already finished primary five and had even passed the common entrance examination that would have enabled her to proceed to secondary school. Anyway, did she have a choice, now that she had come to Ireland to stay? She made up her mind to work hard at her studies and prove to everyone that she was better than that class.

In fact, Ihotu got to love her new school. It was in the neighbourhood where they lived and was only about fifteen minutes' walk from their house. Ene, who was six years old, had done her junior and senior infant classes there and was now about to start first class and Ehi, who had just turned four years, was about to start junior infant class at the same school. With Ihotu now attending the same school, this meant that the school-run was going to be easier for Ebere who already disliked the idea of having to collect Ehi, and then go back a second time to pick up Ene because of their different closing times. She was delighted because she would only need to drive the children to school in the morning and then only have to go back for Ehi. Ene and Ihotu could walk back home as both of them would finish at the same time.

Ihotu was an exceptionally brilliant student. However, when she spoke, her Nigerian accent triggered giggles among her classmates, and this made her become extremely shy and quiet at school. In her class, which had about twenty pupils, there were only two other black children and she was naturally drawn to them. However, as they would often leave her and go to play with their other friends, most days she felt compelled to be on her own and to read a book during break time.

Nevertheless, by the end of that term, her academic performance was so outstanding that it endeared her to her class teacher. It wasn't long before she became fully integrated into school-life and her teacher started involving her in all the class activities and sending her on various errands. Her performance, along with her good behaviour soon gained her recognition in the school. Before the term was over, she observed that her classmates no longer laughed when she spoke, neither was she being asked to speak slowly or to repeat herself. This was because she had gradually picked up an Irish accent. By the time they moved into fifth class, no one seemed to remember that she had joined the school only the previous year.

Chapter 3

The unpleasant experiences of losing her dad at the age of eight and the hardships that she had suffered afterwards with her mum and her siblings before coming to live in Ireland helped to shape Ihotu into a very smart hardworking girl who was determined to succeed. Her well-behaved manner enabled her to easily work her way into the hearts of people whether at school, in their neighbourhood or in their church. Her family attended a Bible church that was located in Dublin City Centre. Most of the people who worshipped there were Africans but there were also a fair number of other races represented and also some Irish people. The pastor was Nigerian. Edache and Ebere were ordained workers in the church; Edache worked in the technical department while Ebere helped with the children.

Ihotu had given her heart to the Lord at the age of seven and loved the Lord dearly. She was happy that her uncle and aunty were also Christians. All the family went to church regularly, and Ihotu became very active in the children's church and always seemed to know more than her peers, especially in the area of reciting Bible verses. This was probably because her mum had got her to memorise one Bible verse every week ever since she was eight years old. That exercise had not made sense to her then as she always seemed to forget the previous verses every time she learnt a new one. Now, she realised the exercise had paid off as she was always winning one prize or another. Whenever there were special programmes for children that involved quiz competitions, Ihotu's team was most likely to beat the other teams. Her Bible knowledge challenged the other children, especially the boys, to work harder as they got tired of either her or her team winning all the prizes.

Edache loved Ihotu dearly and treated her just like his own children, Ene and Ehi. Ebere also got along quite well with her. In fact, the relationship between all of them was very cordial until Ihotu was due to go to secondary school. By then, Ene was going into fourth class and Ehi was going into second. However, Ene and Ehi, were not as smart and hard working as Ihotu and the constant comparisons made by people who thought Ihotu was their older sister soon made them begin to resent her. Sadly, their mum also began to resent her as well.

On the night of Ihotu's Primary School graduation ceremony, her principal, Mr. Brian praised her greatly. He said the school was going to immensely miss her and urged the other pupils to follow her good example. She went home that night with the several prizes that she had won.

Ebere, who had been trying to conceal her resentment for Ihotu, reached her limit when Mr. Brian asked her to come to see him on the Monday following the graduation ceremony. He did this because Ene and Ehi were both causing concern at school because their academic performance was falling behind and there were also reports of misbehaviour from their teachers. He pointed out to her that, in accordance with the school rules, after a child had been punished three times with detention, the next line of action would have to be a suspension. He then expressed his disappointment at how the girls' behaviour was so much in contrast with Ihotu's. Hearing this, Ebere got very angry and blurted out, "You invited me here to talk about my kids, and that is fine with me. But, for heaven's sake, stop comparing them with Ihotu!"

Mr. Brian was surprised at Ebere's reaction and quickly apologised. He said, "Mrs. Edeh, I did not mean to upset you and I apologise for doing so. It's just that coming from the same home; one would expect each of the children to have the same standard of behaviour."

Ebere left Mr. Brian's office that day with her resentment for Ihotu now turned into full-blown hatred. She brooded over the thought that this 'poor, little fatherless girl' that they were trying to help was gradually turning into a star at the expense of her children. She made up her mind to put her in the place where she felt she belonged.

****

Normally, Ihotu would do the chores in the house like washing dishes and doing general cleaning around the house. However, Ebere and her husband had agreed at the beginning of the year that both Ene and Ehi would get more actively involved in those chores, but under Ihotu's supervision. She was instructed to involve the two girls in the washing of dishes and the tidying up of their room. On this particular day, as Ihotu called Ene to come and help with the evening dishes, she was surprised when Ebere shouted at her saying, "What's wrong with your hands? Can't you see that she is doing her homework?" Ihotu tried to explain to her that she was only following their instructions to involve the girls in the housework but this only infuriated Ebere all the more and she shouted, "So you now dare to talk back at me, eh? Just do that one more time and you will see what I will do to you."

Tears dropped from Ihotu's eyes as she quietly went to do the dishes by herself wondering what she had done wrong. Little did she know that Ebere had been nursing resentment against her and that this had gradually turned into hatred and that there was hardly anything she did that pleased her any longer.

This situation progressively got worse until Ebere was picking fault with virtually everything that Ihotu did. Ebere was very shrewd and ensured that her harsh behaviour towards Ihotu was always done when her husband was not around. She would treat Ihotu pleasantly when Edache was at home but behave in a beastly way when he was gone out, and this made things very difficult for Ihotu. The rule in the house was that, if any of the children needed anything, they were to go to Ebere as the person in charge of the house and ask her to provide it for them. With this rule in place, a substantial budget had then been set aside by Edache to cater to the children's needs. As a Health Care Assistant, Ebere only worked one or two nights a week so that she could have time for her. Edache, on the other hand, worked as a Computer Specialist and, as his income was high enough to cater for all the family needs, he didn't bother about Ebere's income when he decided the budget. Even though Ihotu had been included in this budget, Ebere deliberately neglected her needs and would make her ask again and again for basic things such as underwear before she gave her what she needed.

On the other hand, she spent money lavishly on her children. Ihotu began to notice that the clothes Ebere gave her to wear were not new and it wasn't long before she discovered that she was buying them from charity shops that sold used or unwanted items donated to them. She had even bought her secondary school uniforms second-hand from used ones given to the school by some students and parents. The school sells the uniforms to raise funds.

Ebere's attitude not only annoyed Ihotu but it also left her confused. She often wondered how someone could claim to be a born-again Christian and yet live such a double life of pretence and hypocrisy. As she pondered about this, she said to herself, "You should see Aunty Ebere worship and pray in church! Oh, goodness! She could almost bring down the whole church building when she is worshipping God with singing and dancing. She prays the loudest of everybody with a lot of movements and waving of her arms. Anyone who does not know her as I do could think that she is the most spiritual and pious woman in the world. Anyway, I thank God for my mum in whom I saw godly fear. She is a role model for what a Christian woman should be. I will not allow Aunty Ebere to confuse me." Then, Ihotu shook her head as if to shake-off her confusion.

Ihotu's silent suffering continued. She felt she couldn't tell her uncle what his wife did to her when he was not there. She didn't want anything to happen that might ruin their relationship and, moreover, would he even believe her since Ebere was so clever at concealing her ill attitude. She had decided to keep silent about how she was hurting because, at least, she was going to school and her mum had told her that if she focused on her studies she would become a person to be reckoned with in the future. She had also decided to protect the family because they were Christians and for this reason, she wouldn't say anything negative about them to any of her friends or the teachers at school.

****

Ihotu loved basketball and joined the team in her school, a community secondary school in her locality. The school normally had a half day on a Wednesday, which meant that it closed earlier than usual. She had previously asked permission from Ebere to stay after school for a basketball match and had been given consent. She usually got home around half past five in the evening on a Wednesday because of the match and to do so she got on the five o'clock bus. On this particular day, however, the match lasted a bit longer than usual and she missed the bus. As the bus from her school only runs once every hour, this meant that she had to wait to catch the six o'clock bus. She didn't have a phone to call home and explain the change of plan as Ebere had refused to get her another phone after her last one developed a fault and stopped working. She decided to go to the library nearby to study while she waited for the bus. When she finally got home, it was about half past six in the evening. She was surprised to find her uncle home from work and sitting in the living room with his wife.

As soon as they saw her coming in, Edache became furious with her and accused her of hanging around with boys. As she tried to explain what had happened, Ebere joined in, reiterating the accusations against her. Turning to Edache, she said, "Remember what I have been telling you? I'm happy that you can see it for yourself now. Every Wednesday, her school closes at two o'clock, but she doesn't get home until half past five in the evening. I have even seen her hanging around with those boys in the neighbourhood on several occasions. I hope her behaviour doesn't corrupt Ene and Ehi."

Ihotu was shocked and speechless that the same person who had given consent for her to stay behind after school on Wednesdays for basketball practice was now the one telling lies about her. Neither Edache nor Ebere was willing to listen to her explanations. Instead, her uncle warned her sternly to cease such shameful and irresponsible acts. He said that he never wanted to get such a report about her again.

"How could my uncle believe all the lies told by his wife? Why did he not even give me the benefit of the doubt by at least listening to my explanation? Does this mean that Aunty Ebere has constantly been lying to him against me?" These and many similar questions filled Ihotu's mind as she went upstairs to her room, devastated. She slumped on her bed and burst into tears. Any time she was badly treated like this, she would remember her family in Africa and, especially her late dad. This time she sobbed, "How could death be so cruel to me? Oh, Daddy, if only you were alive, then I would not be staying with guardians who falsely accuse me like this." She was still weeping when she heard Ebere screaming her name to come down to the kitchen at once. She washed her face, dried it with a towel and tried to remain calm as she went down to the kitchen to prepare the evening meal.

Ebere seemed to be pleased with herself that she had succeeded in getting her husband to see Ihotu in a bad light. She could see from Ihotu's eyes that she had been crying, but she pretended that everything was alright and tried to appear friendly by telling her light jokes. Ihotu, understanding her game-plan, did her chores quietly and tried to be polite with her. It was now obvious to Ihotu that Ebere didn't like her and so she would just have to be very careful when in her company.

That night, Ihotu could hardly sleep as the events of the day kept replaying in her mind. What she couldn't understand was that Ebere was supposed to be a Christian. How then could she tell such lies with their damaging effect on her and yet carry on as if everything was fine? Sobbing between these thoughts, she eventually fell asleep in the early hours of the following morning, and she had only slept for about three hours when her alarm clock woke her. Feeling exhausted, she made up her mind to quit basketball altogether and any other activity that would require her to stay behind after school.

Chapter 4

"Nine 'A's and two 'B's! Oh, I can't believe it!" Ihotu exclaimed excitedly when she opened the envelope and saw the results of her Junior Certificate Examination that she had sat a couple of months earlier. When she got home and showed the results to Edache, he was very pleased and hugged and congratulated her. Ene and Ehi also hugged her as they joined in the jubilation and Ihotu realised that she hadn't been as happy as this in a long time. "Thank God that all my hard work has paid off," she said to herself as she jumped and danced around the house. She was now almost sixteen years of age and gradually turning into a tall and beautiful young lady. As she stood beside her uncle, he suddenly felt quite short even though he was of average height, as she was now slightly taller than him and he wondered how fast children could grow. Edache popped open a bottle of wine to celebrate her success.

The Junior Cert examination is a national examination that students in Ireland take at the end of their first three years in secondary school.

Based on their performance, they can then proceed to the senior level where they have the option to study subjects of their own choice. In this exam, Ihotu had sat the higher level papers. A student can take either the ordinary or the higher level papers, and the latter are very challenging as an 'A' in a subject represents a score of 85% and above.

Edache and the girls were still celebrating when Ebere came in. She had been out all day and was surprised to see everyone in such a festive mood. "What's happening here?" she asked and had repeated the question for the third time before she got anyone's attention. The girls were all talking at the same time making it more difficult to grasp anything until Edache quietened them down and shared Ihotu's good news with her. She merely replied coldly, "Is that all? I thought one of you had won the Lottery! Congratulations, Ihotu" and with that, she went upstairs to her room.

They continued the celebration anyway. Edache announced that he was ordering pizza for everyone and the girls all went hysterical. "Kids and take-away food!" Edache muttered to himself. "There is so much food at home which sometimes even gets thrown away, yet when I mention fast-food, they behave as if they haven't eaten in weeks." The pizza he ordered was delivered about thirty minutes later, and they happily devoured it. By the time they had finished eating it was time to go to bed. Edache sent everyone to their rooms after they had said their night prayers and then he went to his room.

Edache noticed that his wife had a very cold attitude that night. She had neither joined them in the celebration nor in the night prayers.

"Are you ok?" he asked as he stepped into the room and saw her lying on the bed with her face towards the wall.

"Yeah, I'm just tired," she replied.

"Is that why you didn't join us for dinner or night prayers?" he enquired.

"Yes! I said I am tired!" she said. Her reply this time was quite sharp and, at this, Edache decided to drop the issue because he noticed that she was not in a very good mood. She remained unusually quiet all that night. Edache waited to see if her mood would change but then eventually went to sleep.

****

Next morning, it was time for school and Ihotu, having assisted Ene and Ehi to get ready, was set to leave for school herself when Ebere came into the kitchen.

"Aunty, good morning" Ihotu greeted her. Without answering, Ebere angrily demanded, "Is this how you are going to leave the kitchen in this mess and go to school?"

"I'm sorry, Aunty," Ihotu replied. "But I can't tidy up while Ene and Ehi are still eating and if I don't leave now, I will miss my bus."

Ebere raised her voice as she retorted, "How dare you talk to me like that!" The next thing Ihotu knew was that Ebere had landed a slap on her face, shouting, "Who do you think you are? "Oh, is it because your Junior Cert results were so good and everyone was fussing around you yesterday that you've forgotten who you are, eh? So now you are too big to clean the house? And you even dare to use my children as your excuse. By the way, that slap is just a taster. If you don't learn how to talk and behave yourself in this house, then more such slaps will be coming your way. And let me warn you that if you step out of this house without cleaning up first, then don't bother to come back!" With that, Ebere turned and stormed out of the kitchen.

"Mum! That was mean!" Ehi shouted after her.

"And it is child abuse," Ene added loudly.

Their mum shouted back at them to be quiet as she walked to her room.

Ihotu felt so bad, and with tears in her eyes, she dropped her school-bag and began to clean the kitchen. Ene and Ehi came around her trying to show her some sympathy and asked, "Ihotu, are you okay?" She hugged them and quietly told them, "It's okay; you just go and finish your breakfast." The girls were particularly slow eaters, and she knew that she could not finish the cleaning until they were finished eating and so she worked slowly while she waited for them to finish at their own pace. She did not want to incur the wrath of Aunty Ebere again by hurrying them up.

Even though Ihotu knew that the reason for Ebere's angry outburst went beyond the kitchen not being tidied up and was probably because of her great exam results and the way her uncle had celebrated her success; she couldn't help but wonder, "Is she jealous of me or does my success infuriate or intimidate her in some way? Why does she hate me so much? As my guardian, should she not be pleased with my success? After all, a lot of the credit would go to her for bringing me up well. Aunty Ebere is old enough to be my mother, so I cannot understand why my success seems to upset her like this."

By the time she finished the chores, thirty minutes had gone by, and Ihotu knew that her bus would have gone as well. The next bus wasn't due until another twenty-five minutes, and although it would take her only about ten minutes to walk to the bus-stop, she decided that she would prefer to wait there in the cold for the bus rather than stay alone in the house with Ebere. Ene and Ehi had already left for school by this time, while her uncle had left for work before the whole incident started. She arrived in school late that day and missed the first class. She did not say anything about the incident to anyone but instead tried to look calm. She just told her class teacher that she had missed the bus.

Ihotu was now in the fifth year because she had decided to skip Transition Year (TY). TY is an optional fourth year in secondary schools in Ireland. It is a less stressful year for the students as they are given the opportunity to unwind following the stress of the Junior Cert Exam. During this year, the students can try out different subjects before deciding which ones they want to study for the Leaving Certificate Exams. The students also have an opportunity to do some work experience that may relate to the fields of their desired future careers, as well as go on exciting school trips. It is the academic year with the most fun.

Ihotu, with the consent of her uncle, decided to skip TY because she felt that she had lost enough time related to her schooling due to her relocation to Ireland. She was now sixteen years old and some of her friends back in Nigeria who were the same age as she were already in the university. She wanted to get through with her secondary school education and proceed to college as soon as possible. Fun or no fun, she had decided that TY was not for her. As she had selected seven subjects to study for her Leaving Cert Exams including Irish, she was determined to get at least six 'A's. She was not particularly fond of the Irish Language and didn't expect to perform very well in that particular exam.

****

Ihotu was thrilled when she returned home from school the day after she had received her Junior Cert results, and her uncle had the gift of a new mobile phone for her. She was so excited! For over a year now, she had managed without a phone of her own. Her last one had broken, and Ebere wasn't willing to replace it for her. Due to not having a phone of her own, she hadn't been able to pour out her heart to her mum the way she would have liked. The only time she got an opportunity to talk to her mum was when her mum called Edache, and in that kind of atmosphere, she felt that she couldn't talk heart to heart with her. So, the first person she rang as soon as she got upstairs was her mum to give her the new number. Now that Edache had bought some credit for her new phone, she decided that she had better let her mum know her number so that she could call her back anytime she wanted. Anyway, she didn't intend to discuss much now. She would just give her the number and let her know the best times to call her, which she imagined would be during a break at school.

While Ihotu was rejoicing over her phone, she overheard Ehi saying to her dad, "Mummy slapped Ihotu today." Edache, shocked at this news, called her to confirm if it was true. Before she could say anything, Ene began to narrate the whole incident. When Ihotu nodded and confirmed that it was true, Uncle Edache assured her that he would get to the bottom of the issue and sort everything out.

Ihotu's recent results had stirred Edache's heart and softened his feelings towards her again. In truth, he loved her, but the constant negative reports that his wife gave him about her had made him very harsh in his treatment of her. He wondered, "Why would Ebere slap her because of a minor issue such as not cleaning up the kitchen before leaving for school? How would it be possible for her to clean up when she needed to leave for school before their kids who were usually not finished by the time she was due to leave?"

In fact, this news made Edache begin to think seriously. He realised that Ihotu had not even mentioned a word about the incident to him by herself! He probably would not have known anything about it if Ehi and Ene had not told him. He wondered, "Have I been misjudging her? If Ihotu were really hanging around with boys and doing all the things that Ebere had accused her of, could she have done so well in her studies?" He often found it difficult to know who was telling the truth any time Ebere accused her and her, on the other hand, was denying the allegations vehemently. He recalled that Ihotu had never told him anything that he later discovered to be a lie, but he still couldn't understand why his wife would say she had done something if she did not do it. "The situation between the two of them can be very confusing!" He said to himself. "I love my wife, and I trust her, but I also love Ihotu, and I have taken her into my home like a daughter." With that, he bowed his head and prayed, "God, please help me to be more discerning, and to resolve this issue amicably." He made up his mind to watch Ihotu more closely from then on to confirm certain things for himself. He also resolved, in the meantime, to have a discussion with Ebere on the issue.

That night, after the children had gone to bed, Edache raised the issue with Ebere. "Oh, sweetheart," Ebere said apologetically, "I'm so sorry, I just lost my temper because of the way she was talking rudely to me."

"Honey," Edache replied, "you know the laws in this country. What if Ihotu reported this incident to the authorities? I would like you to be more careful in the future as I don't want this kind of incident to happen again."

"Okay, I promise. It will never happen again," said Ebere. Then she added jokingly, "I even cross my heart." And they both laughed and dropped the subject. Edache felt convinced that his wife did not mean any harm towards Ihotu.

However, Ebere was thinking to herself, "Now that this report has got to my husband, I will have to be more subtle in my dealings with this girl. I don't want him to get any clue that I hate her. So, from now on, I am going to make sure that I have a tangible proof for anything I say about her."

Chapter 5

Ebere, in her cunning way, had resolved to make things difficult for Ihotu and she seemed to be succeeding with her plans. Ihotu, on the other hand, was trying very hard to do everything she knew to please her, but it appeared that the more she tried, the more Ebere frustrated her efforts.

Ihotu woke up very early one morning, an hour earlier than usual. She vacuumed the entire house and made Ebere's favourite breakfast. She also ensured that Ene and Ehi were ready on time for school. She was so sure that her aunty would at least smile at her even if she didn't verbalise her appreciation, but she was to be totally disappointed. By all appearances, Ebere did not even notice one thing she had done, and as soon as she came downstairs, even though everywhere was spotlessly clean, she walked into the living-room, lifted the curtains and started complaining.

"Ihotu, have I not always told you to open the windows every time you vacuum, to let in some

fresh air? One can hardly breathe in this room!"
she said as she opened the windows.

"But Aunty, the weather is very cold, and
remember, you always said we should keep the
doors and windows shut when the heater was
on, to keep the house warm," Ihotu replied.

"Can't you use your common sense?" Ebere
snapped back. "Anyway, I should have known
that common sense does not grow in everyone's
garden." From there, Ebere walked into the
kitchen where Ehi and Ene were having their
breakfast, and she picked on Ihotu again. "Why
did you allow Ehi to wear this shirt? Can't you
see that it is rumpled?"

"Aunty, I ironed that shirt over the weekend, and
she just wore it yesterday. She is only wearing it
for the second time today," Ihotu answered.

Ebere, seeing something covered up on the table,
went over and looked to see what it was. It was
'Akara' (bean cake) and custard that Ihotu had
prepared for her. Instead of thanking her she
said, "How come you have the time to make
Akara on a Tuesday morning when you should
be busy doing more important things?"

"Aunty, I was only trying to please you by
preparing your favourite breakfast for you,"

Ihotu explained. Then she walked out of the kitchen heading for the stairs to go up to her room.

Ebere was enraged because she felt that Ihotu had walked out on her. "So, you are walking out on me, eh?" she yelled as she rushed after Ihotu to pull her back. Ihotu was already on the stairs by the time that Ebere got near her, and as she reached out to grab her, she tripped and fell backward scraping her hand and her face against a rough part of the wall near the staircase. As she fell to the floor, her head hit it, and she cried out in pain. Hearing her scream, Ene and Ehi rushed to her side asking, "Mum, are you okay?" They began to cry as they looked at her lying there on the floor, groaning in pain and with blood flowing from a wound on her head.

Ihotu also ran down to her, shocked and confused by what had just happened. "Oh, Aunty, I'm sorry," she said not knowing what to do to help her. So many questions came to her all at once. "Should I give her First Aid? Should I call an ambulance? Oh, what will I do now?" she wondered. Then she said out loud, "Will I call an ambulance?" However, no one seemed to be paying any attention to her, so she picked up the house phone, rang the emergency number and asked for an ambulance. As she waited for the ambulance to arrive, she suddenly remembered to ring her uncle and tell him what had happened.

Edache worked in Dublin City Centre and liked to commute to work by train. His train was near the City Centre when Ihotu's call came through to him. He was alarmed and shocked by her news and wished he had come in his car so that he could turn back to go home immediately. Unfortunately, he had to wait until the train got to his stop which was the next one. He got off and made his way directly to the platform where he could catch the next train back home, only to discover that it wasn't due to leave for another twenty minutes. So, instead of just standing there waiting for it, he thought it wiser to at least go to his work-place, which was only five minutes away, so that he could clock in and also obtain permission to leave and go back home. He felt agitated as he didn't seem to be in control of anything that was happening at the moment. He chose not to drive to work each day because of the cost of parking in the City Centre. It was an expense he felt he could avoid. And, moreover, taking the train helped him avoid the stress of driving in the rush-hour traffic. Instead, he could relax during the journey each day as he commuted to and from work. However, this had turned out to be one of those days when these advantages seemed insignificant. He needed to get home, and he wanted to get there as soon as possible!

The ambulance arrived about twenty-five minutes after the call and Ebere was rushed to the hospital. Ihotu was torn between accompanying her in the ambulance and staying with the girls, but then Ebere told her to stay at home with them. Ihotu held the two girls, one at her left side and the other at her right. With tears in their eyes, they watched the ambulance drive Ebere off to the hospital. Then the three of them retired to the sitting room and slumped into the couch. Ihotu couldn't help wondering if she was responsible for the accident. She battled with feelings of guilt, and she kept saying to herself, "If only I had known that she was going to run after me, I would not have walked away in the first place." On the other hand, she knew that if she hadn't walked away just then, she would probably have said or done something else that Ebere would have used against her. She was still lost in her thoughts when Edache arrived home about an hour later.

"What happened to my wife? Where is she?" Edache demanded as he rushed into the house. When he heard that Ebere had been taken to hospital in an ambulance, he asked Ihotu for the name of the hospital. She told him the name given her by the ambulance driver, and then he grabbed his car keys to rush over there as quickly as he could. "Can we come?" Ihotu, Ene, and Ehi asked almost simultaneously. Edache shook his head and told them that he needed to go there first to see what the situation was and then he would come back for them later.

Edache got to the hospital to find Ebere still waiting in the Accident and Emergency (A&E) Unit, yet to be seen by a doctor. A triage nurse had examined her and assessed her case as serious but not critical. As the A&E unit was always jam-packed, yet under-staffed, only someone very seriously ill, maybe near the point of death would be considered a critical case to be seen immediately by a doctor. All other cases no matter how serious had to wait for a while, and patients sometimes had to wait for up to eight hours or even more before been seen by a doctor in this particular A&E unit. The amount of time one had to wait depends on how serious the triage nurse rated the person's illness. The less serious your illness, the longer you had to wait before been seen by a doctor.

"Honey, what happened? Are you okay?" Edache asked as he ran to his wife. Before Ebere could say anything, he asked her more questions. "When did you get here? Why haven't they attended to you?"

When Ebere told him that she had been there for over an hour, Edache decided to go and find out from a member of staff when a doctor would be available to examine his wife. He wanted to make them understand the seriousness of her condition. The staff he spoke to replied: "Mr. Edache, I understand your concern, but I also want you to realise that there are people here with cases equally serious, and some, even more serious than that of your wife. Some of them have been here for more than three hours. We are doing our best to make sure all the patients are attended to as soon as possible." Edache felt like telling her that their best efforts were not good enough, but he decided to hold his peace and go back to his wife.

"So, what happened?" he asked Ebere as he settled into the seat beside her.

"It was Ihotu o," Ebere replied.

"Ihotu? What about Ihotu?" Edache asked, not understanding where the conversation was heading.

"I hope that girl will not kill me one day," Ebere added.

Edache now getting impatient demanded: "Can you just get straight to the point and tell me, what has Ihotu got to do with you being in the hospital?"

Ebere, sensing that she had got him to the point where he was eager to listen to her, went on to narrate her story. "I came downstairs this morning when Ihotu and the girls were almost ready for school, and I noticed that the house was dusty and stuffy. So, I told Ihotu that the next time she vacuumed the house and it got stuffy like that, she should open the windows for a while for some ventilation. Apparently, this did not go down well with her as she rudely told me that I never appreciate anything she does but, instead I am always trying to find fault with her work. While I was still talking to her, trying to explain that, as much as I appreciate her, there is also a need to correct her so that she can grow up to be a responsible person, then she walked out on me. I tried calling her back, but she wouldn't listen. So, I decided to go after her, still trying to reason with her. The next thing I knew, I was on the floor, bleeding. She had pushed me angrily from behind her down the stairs, telling me to go to hell. Hmm...." She concluded with a sigh that portrays deep agony.

When Edache heard Ebere's story, he was mad. "What! Is this some form of a joke or something? Honey, I know you are not joking, but what could have come over Ihotu to make her behave like this? Anyway, whatever it is, I am going to make that girl come to her senses!" Edache was shaking with anger and would have gone home immediately to deal with Ihotu if it weren't for his wife's condition.

"Sweetheart, please calm down," Ebere cautioned her husband, "I don't want your blood pressure to go up because of this. She is only a young girl and probably does not know the implication of what she was doing." However, Ebere was inwardly pleased as she knew that Ihotu wasn't going to have it easy with her uncle on this occasion. "I will see how she will escape this one." She thought to herself as she tried to calm her husband down.

Edache, on the other hand, was overwhelmed by deep thoughts as he tried to understand what could have come over Ihotu. The Ihotu he knew wouldn't normally behave like that or say such nasty words. He felt so disappointed and ashamed of the whole situation that he didn't want to talk about it any longer.

"Ebere Edeh!" a voice called. It was now Ebere's turn to be seen by a doctor. After asking her a series of questions, the doctor examined her and sent her for some X-rays to make sure that she hadn't broken any bones. Thankfully, the X-ray results showed that everything was fine. However, after further tests, the doctor decided that she should be kept in the hospital overnight for observation. It was evening by the time they were ready to admit her, and when she had settled in, Edache was advised to go home.

When Edache got home, he was furious and the way he stormed into the house both surprised and frightened Ihotu. The two girls were asleep at this time. Ihotu had stayed awake, waiting to know the outcome of his going to the hospital. "How is Aunty? Is she alright?" Ihotu asked as she got up to welcome him. Rather than answer her, he grabbed her and threw her on to the couch, shouting at her, "What did you do to my wife?"

Ihotu had never seen her uncle this angry. Almost scared to death, she replied, "Uncle, I don't understand. I didn't do anything to her." He then asked another question, "Did your aunty tell you to open the windows when she came down this morning because the house was stuffy?"

"Yes," Ihotu replied, "but......"

"But what?" Edache barked at her. "Did you walk out on her while she was still talking to you?"

"Uncle, it wasn't like that at all. I was getting late for school, and I thought she had finished talking to me when I left to go upstairs" Ihotu replied.

"Okay, one more question. Did you tell her that she never appreciates what you do?"

"Yes, I did, and that is because...."

"Because of what? Edache interrupted before Ihotu could finish. "You have an explanation for everything. You dare to be rude to my wife, walk out on her, push her down the stairs and even tell her to go to hell?"

"No, uncle. That's not true. I never told her to go hell, and I never pushed her down the stairs," Ihotu said with tears in her eyes.

"So, my wife is now a liar. Is that it?" Edache snapped.

"No uncle, I didn't say that. You are getting the whole thing wrong."

"Oh, you mean that I am stupid, and I cannot understand things *eh*?" said Edache as he interrupted her again before she could finish speaking.

"Uncle, how could I ever say or even think such a thing about you? Aunty Ebere tripped and fell. I would never have pushed her or said any nasty words to her. Uncle, please believe me," Ihotu said. By now she was crying profusely.

"Will you be quiet and stop shedding those crocodile tears," Edache shouted at her. If it weren't for the promise I made to my sister, your mother, I would throw you out of my house this very night." Edache said as he stormed out of the room and headed upstairs.

When he had gone, Ihotu broke down completely and wept all the more. It was bad and painful enough for Ebere to accuse her of pushing her down the stairs and even lying that she had told her 'to go to hell'. What was even more devastating for her was the fact that her uncle did not wait to hear her out fully, and yet he believed all that had been said against her by his wife. After sobbing her heart out, she eventually dozed off on the couch. She was later jerked up by cold in the middle of the night, and she was surprised to find she had been sleeping on the sofa in the sitting-room. Now awake, the memory of all that had happened the previous day came rushing back to her and tears welled up in her eyes again as she got up to go to her room.

In the morning, Edache still wanting to get to the bottom of what had transpired between his wife and Ihotu called Ene and Ehi to ask them their version of what had happened. Ene explained, "Mummy was talking to Ihotu, then Ihotu left to go upstairs, and Mummy followed her. The next thing we heard from the kitchen was Mummy screaming. Ehi and I ran out, and we saw Mummy on the floor, and she was bleeding." On hearing what the girls had to say, Edache was convinced that Ihotu did walk out on his wife and push her down the stairs. He made up his mind to get very tough with her from then on.

Chapter 6

Ebere was discharged from the hospital the next day when the doctor confirmed that despite the cuts and bruises she had obtained there was no internal injury. With the painkillers, she was given she felt much better and wasn't hurting so badly anymore. Her homecoming was an exciting moment for the whole family if it weren't for the fact that she decided to ignore Ihotu and would not even respond to her greeting.

Later that evening, Edache called a meeting, where the entire family including Ihotu were present. At the meeting, he apologised to his wife for Ihotu's bad behaviour which he said was his fault. Then he asked her to apologise to Ebere. Ihotu knelt down to apologise but, instead of words, all that came from her were tears. Apologising was not difficult for her to do, but she found it very difficult to accept the blame for what she had not done. Eventually, she managed to say sorry, and her uncle told her to get up. Edache then announced his disciplinary agenda for her which meant that Ebere would be totally in charge of everything to do with her. He added that in future, he would never interfere with how Ebere chose to raise and discipline her.

Turning to her, he said sternly, "By this, Ihotu, you will learn to submit to your aunty and respect her." With that, he ended the meeting.

Ihotu had already missed two days of school that week and was looking forward to going back the following day. At least, it would give her a chance to get away from home for some hours. She was also looking forward to catching up with her school-work which had suffered over these few days as well. However, Ebere had a different agenda for her. In the morning, after Ihotu had made sure that the two girls were ready for school and was set to leave for her school, she heard Ebere calling her from upstairs. She ran to Ebere's room thinking something was wrong only to find her lying on the bed, snuggled up under her duvet.

"Get some hot water and come massage my shoulders," Ebere ordered her.

Ihotu was shocked at this instruction as Ebere could see that she was already dressed in her school uniform and about to leave for school. She opened her mouth to speak but quickly closed it again out of fear.

"Did you not hear me?" Ebere shouted at her.

"Yes, Aunty," Ihotu replied and went quickly to get the water ready. As she was coming upstairs with the bowl of water and a towel to do the massage, Ebere overheard Ene and Ehi's voices arguing downstairs, and she yelled at Ihotu, "What are those girls still doing at home? Shouldn't they be in school by now?

Before Ihotu could answer her, Ebere told her to go back downstairs and make sure that the girls were ready to leave. She added that she should walk Ehi to her school and go with Ene to her bus stop.

"Since when did this start?" Ihotu wondered silently. Ehi's school was just a few minutes' walk down the road from their house. She was now in fifth class and had been going to school by herself ever since Ene entered secondary school. Ene, on the other hand, was now in first year in secondary school and got a private bus at a stop near Ehi's school. However, Ihotu did not dare argue with Ebere. She quietly placed the bowl of water and the towel in the corner of her room and went back downstairs to check on Ene and Ehi. When she informed them that she would be walking Ehi to school and Ene to her bus stop that morning, they both protested.

"Ihotu, we're not babies," Ehi stated.

"I know you are not babies but having your older cousin walking beside you is not going to do you any harm," Ihotu answered.

"Ihotu, you don't have to bother. You know we can get to school by ourselves," Ene added.

When they saw that Ihotu wouldn't relent and was determined to walk them to school and the bus stop, Ene asked with concern: "Won't you be late for your school then?" Ihotu told them not to worry, that she would be fine. Hearing this, they relaxed and off they went, chatting all the way.

As soon as Ihotu got back home and showed up in Ebere's room, Ebere yelled at her, "How did it take you so long to get back? Anyway, I'm sure the water you brought up will be cold by now so go and get fresh hot water." Ihotu went for the water and was back in a few minutes to do the massage. As she tried to gently massage Ebere's shoulders, Ebere, between screams and abusive words, continued to give out to her. Ihotu managed to finish the massage and thought she would be free for a while, but Ebere told her to go and get breakfast ready for her. And so, it was one chore after the other and it made Ihotu miss school all that day.

At the end of the day, when Ihotu retired to bed, she couldn't help but weep, wondering how long this situation was going to continue. Then, she quietly prayed to God to make way for her to finish her secondary education and to also proceed to college. She remembered her mum's words that "A good education will give you a strong foundation in life." She also wondered how different her life would have been if her dad were still alive. Eventually, she went to sleep.

****

Next morning, Ihotu woke up, not sure of what Ebere's agenda for the day was going to be. It was Friday, and she had prayed and hoped that her aunty would let her go to school. She did her usual house-chores, and when she had finished, she went up to Ebere's room to check on her. Ebere, even though awake was still in bed. "Aunty, good morning," Ihotu greeted her and went on to ask, "Are you feeling any better this morning?" She could hardly hear Ebere's reply, so she asked gently: "Is there anything you want me to do for you before I go to school?" Ebere didn't expect this level of calmness and concern from her, and so she asked if Ehi & Ene were ready for school and if the house had been tidied up. When Ihotu answered in the affirmative, Ebere said she could leave. Ihotu was thrilled to be able to go back to school again after being at home for several days. "God surely does answer prayers!" she said to herself. "He has granted my heart's desire and made a way for me to be back in school."

At school, Ihotu discovered that there was a huge backlog of her school-work, including various assignments, waiting to be done. She had missed quite a lot in those few days. She hated falling behind, and so she resolved to catch up as soon as possible. She decided to use any spare time she had that day in school, including her break-time, to begin the work she would need to do to catch up. She considered her education to be the primary reason for her being in Ireland, and she was determined to get the most out of it. The day went quite quickly and, before she knew it, it was time to go home. The mere thought of going back home frightened her as she was uncertain of what would await her this time. Ebere had become very unpredictable, and she had a way of influencing Edache and even the two girls against her.

Ihotu's plans to catch up with her school-work that weekend seemed like a mirage. On this particular Saturday, Ebere kept her busy with house-chores as far as she possibly could. She was normally up by six o'clock every morning, and Ebere did not allow her to have any free time until about ten o'clock that night when it was bedtime. Even though she was exhausted by this time, she still had to sit up in her room and spend an hour or two doing her studies before finally retiring to bed. This turned out to be the regular pattern for her most weekends. Although a lot of people dread Mondays because they have to go back to work or school, Ihotu looked forward to them as it meant spending less time at home.

****

It was another Monday morning. Having finished her usual house-chores, Ihotu was ready to go to school and asked Ebere for her bus-pass for the week. Normally, Ebere would give her a pre-paid bus-pass that enabled her to travel by the public bus to school. On this occasion, however, Ebere flared up at her request, "What bus-pass are talking about? Is it only now you are telling me that you need a bus-pass?"

"Aunty, remember, I reminded you on Friday when I came home from school that my bus-pass was finished," Ihotu replied.

"I don't remember you saying anything like that, and so I don't have a bus-pass to give you," Ebere told her.

"Okay, Aunty, can you give me some money then so that I can stop by the shop and buy myself one before proceeding to the bus stop?" Ihotu asked.

With that, Ebere shouted at her to get out of her presence. "You can stay at home today if you think you cannot get to school without a bus-pass," she added.

Ihotu was stunned. "Okay, Aunty, I will walk," she said and headed to get her school-bag and her jacket.

The weather that morning was extremely cold, and only God knew how long it would take her to walk to school! She had already missed so much the previous week and was still trying to catch up, and so she was determined not to allow the lack of a bus-pass to prevent her from getting to school. Anyway, she felt it was better to get out of the house by whatever means than to stay at home with Ebere, especially now that her uncle had gone to work, and the girls had gone to their schools.

Ihotu was humming a song to herself as she walked down the road. She was hardly out of her estate when she heard a car-horn beeping at her. She couldn't believe her eyes. It was Laura and her dad. Laura was a girl in her school that lived in the same estate as she did. The car stopped, and Laura wound down her window and asked her if she would like a lift to school.

"Yes, please," said Ihotu as she happily hurried into the car and they drove off. "Laura asked me if I would like a lift?" she said to herself. "I actually, desperately needed this lift!"

Like Ihotu, Laura normally went to school by bus, but as she explained, she wasn't feeling too well, and her dad decided to give her a lift. Ihotu considered the help they gave her to be a miracle. She was so grateful to Laura and her dad, but also to God.

What happened that morning reminded Ihotu of events in the Bible where God made a way when there seemed to be no way. It not only encouraged her to continue to trust God, but it also brightened up her whole day, and she went about her activities that day joyfully, thanking God every time she remembered the incident. It was only when school was over that she remembered that she didn't have any means of getting back home.

When Aoife, a girl that Ihotu usually hung out with in school, met with her so that they could walk to the bus-stop together, she noticed that Ihotu was dragging her feet. She told her to hurry up so that they wouldn't miss the bus. She also noticed that Ihotu was being unusually quiet and was not responding to her prompting and so she asked her, "Ihotu, are you alright?"

"Yeah" Ihotu answered quietly.

"So then why are you being so quiet and slow?" Aoife asked.

"Aoife, you can go ahead. I'm not going home by bus today," Ihotu told her.

"Are you getting a lift off someone then?" Aoife probed further.

At this point, Ihotu had to tell her that she wasn't going on the bus because she didn't have a bus-pass.

"Oh, Ihotu!" Aoife exclaimed. "Why didn't you tell me? I have a spare one with me. My mum got me a new bus-pass this morning, and I think I still have one or two journeys left on my old one. So you can have it."

"Are you serious? Ihotu exclaimed excitedly, her face brightening up.

"What are friends for?" Aoife asked as she handed her the bus-pass and they both hurried off to catch the bus.

"God has provided for me once again," Ihotu said to herself, quietly rejoicing in her heart as the two of them walked to the bus stop.

Ebere was quite surprised to see Ihotu come back at her usual time. She had expected her to arrive home very late since she didn't have a bus-pass and would have had to walk home. As soon as Ihotu entered the house and greeted her, she literally jumped at her and said "I thought you said you didn't have a bus-pass. So how did you get to school and then back on time?"

Ihotu explained to her that Laura and her dad had given her a lift on her way to school and that on the way home her friend Aoife had given her an old bus pass with just one or two journeys left on it.

"You're a liar!" said Ebere. "How can I be sure that it was the school you went to today and not to your boyfriend's house?"

"Aunty, I don't have a boyfriend, and I am not lying. I can show you the work we did in school today," said Ihotu.

"Eh.....you can keep your lies and deception to yourself," Ebere retorted as she walked away from her.

"What kind of person is this? How can someone who claims to be a Christian be so mean and so wicked?" Ihotu thought as she stood there, speechless. She decided to let it pass and go find something to eat. It had been a very busy and also a very exciting day, a day she had been so joyful because of the way she had experienced the faithfulness of God. She made up her mind that she wasn't going to let Ebere ruin it for her. After all, God had out-smarted Ebere on this day, and that strengthened her faith in Him and gave her hope for the days ahead.

The following day, Ebere still refused to give Ihotu a bus-pass. "What am I going to do?" Ihotu wondered. "The bus-pass Aoife gave me yesterday has only one journey left on it. That can take me to school but how am I going to get back home?" She continued to wonder. She made up her mind not to do anything stupid, especially something that would be against her Christian ethics to get money. Finally, she concluded and said to herself, "God provided for me yesterday, and so He can still provide for me today. If He doesn't provide transport for me today, then He must want me to have the experience of walking home." With that in mind, she felt encouraged and set out for school. She was humming the song, "The joy of the Lord is my strength" to herself as she walked to the bus-stop and used the last journey on the bus-pass that her friend Aoife had given her.

Things at school went smoothly that day, but from time to time, whenever Ihotu thought about how she would get home, she would start to panic. Then, every time she felt like that, she quickly encouraged herself with a verse from the Bible that seemed to simultaneously come into her mind. This continued until it was time for her to leave. As usual, Aoife met up with her for the two of them to walk together to the bus stop. As they approached it, she told Aoife that she would have to walk home this time because, once again, she didn't have a bus-pass.

Aoife was furious! "You mean your aunty still hasn't bought you a bus-pass or given you the money to buy one? How does she expect you to get to school and then come back home? Does she seriously expect you to walk the long distance home in this cold? Honestly, Ihotu, I think you should report this aunty of yours to a social worker or the *Gardai* (Police in Ireland). What she is doing to you is called child-abuse, and she would be in serious trouble for treating you like this! After all, she collects the children's allowance on your behalf, doesn't she?"

"Ah... no...," Ihotu protested, "I don't want her to get into trouble because of me. I would rather depend on God to make way for me."

"Do you think God is going to come down and stop this abuse?" said Aoife. "I hate to see people mistreating other people. I know what I am going to do. I am going to ring a social worker and report this case myself on your behalf," she added.

On hearing this, Ihotu started begging her, "Aoife, please don't do that. If you want us to continue being friends, then I beg you. Please stay out of this; it is a family affair, and I will be fine."

"What's the matter with you, Ihotu? Why are you going through what you don't have to go through?" Aoife asked. "Anyway, this aunty of yours should be thankful that she doesn't have someone like me as a niece! She would have gotten a double dose back for all her trouble. Anyway, because it's you, I will keep quiet this time around but, if things don't change soon, I'll be forced to speak out." And Ihotu thanked her for being an understanding friend.

"I have some cash with me. I can pay your bus-fare home," Aoife offered.

"Oh, no," Ihotu said. "You have done more than enough for me. I want to walk home today and see how long it takes me."

"No, I won't allow you to do that," Aoife said. "I insist on paying your bus-fare," she added emphatically.

"Well, I insist on walking home," Ihotu replied with a smile.

They argued about this for a while until, in the end, Aoife gave up. "Sometimes I don't understand why you like to suffer," she added.

"You worry too much about me, Aoife. I am fine, and I will be fine," said Ihotu.

At this, they hugged each other, and Aoife boarded the bus while Ihotu set out to walk home.

When she finally got home, it was about seven o'clock in the evening. It had taken her more than two hours to walk the distance home. She was happy that she had been able to make it even with the cold weather and the fact that it had already gotten dark before she stepped into the house. It felt so good to step into a warm, bright building. All that had been on her mind as she walked home was getting a hot cup of tea to warm herself up before settling down to eat her evening meal. However, just as she stepped into the house, she heard Edache shout her name, and calling her to come immediately.

When she entered the living-room, Edache was sitting there with Ebere. They had obviously been talking about her before she came in.

"Where are you coming from at this hour?" Edache asked her sternly.

"From the school," Ihotu replied

"At this time of the day?" Ebere queried.

With that, Edache began to scold her, saying many nasty things to her. He said he didn't want her to ruin his children by her waywardness and that she should not bring shame on him or his family. He even went on to say that he had heard a report that she wasn't coming from school but her boyfriend's house.

Ihotu couldn't hold back at this point, and she blurted out, "Uncle, what you are saying to me is not fair. You asked me where I was coming from and I told you. You didn't bother to ask me why I am coming home this late, and now you are accusing me of waywardness. It took me more than two hours to walk home in the cold because I was not given a bus-pass and yet it is still used against me. Is it because I don't have a father any more that you people are doing this to me?" Then she burst into tears, crying profusely.

"Who are the 'you people' that you are referring to?" demanded Ebere as she joined in. Then turning to Edache she said, "Honey are you going to just sit there, and let this small girl insult us like this, and accuse us of been unjust?" She said the 'small girl' with a sneer as a way of belittling Ihotu.

Edache, being a typical African man considered Ihotu's response to him as being very disrespectful. It is against African culture for a child to talk back to an adult in the way that Ihotu had just blurted out. This, along with the negative reports that his wife had given him about Ihotu made him very angry with her.

"How dare you speak back to me in that manner! Am I not a father to you?" Edache demanded as he stood up to face her.

"Uncle, if you really were a father to me, then you would properly investigate any allegation against me before accepting it as true," Ihotu replied.

Ihotu was shocked by the sudden boldness that came upon her enabling her to speak to her uncle like this. She was usually a very shy, quiet and obedient girl and so she didn't know where this boldness came from. Could it be that her uncle and his wife had pushed her too far? She hated lies and would never lie against anyone, and so it pained her deeply that she was being lied against, especially by people whom she looked up to.

Edache was even more shocked at Ihotu's reaction. He had never seen her react this way to anyone. However, instead of believing her, he chose to believe that all Ebere had been saying about her must be true. He reasoned, "If Ihotu weren't hanging out with people who were negatively influencing her, then where did she get the guts to talk back to me like this?" He also wondered, "Could she also have started taking some hard drugs?" He concluded to himself, "Anyway if she has decided to ruin herself then I am not going to allow that. I will do everything possible to bring her back to her right senses." So, he decided that the best way to do this was to make things very difficult for her.

In all honesty, Edache meant well for his niece, but because of the distance between them due to him spending hardly any time with her, he fell for his wife's plot to paint Ihotu *'black'* in his sight. The voice that you hear most often is the one that you are eventually likely to believe. Consciously, or unconsciously, it can also become a powerful driving force in your life! Edache, perhaps unconsciously, was now being driven by the malicious plans of his wife yet he thought that he was doing things for Ihotu's good.

Ebere, in her usual shrewd way, gave Ihotu a bus-pass the very next day so that her scheme would not be exposed.

Chapter 7

The relationship between Ihotu and her uncle continued to sour as each of her movements was viewed with suspicion. Things got more and more difficult for Ihotu as Ebere deprived her of things that would meet her basic needs. By now, she was in her sixth year and very soon would be sitting for her Leaving Certificate Examination. As living with her uncle and his family in Ireland was no longer pleasurable, she decided that the only thing that would make her happy and justify the years that she had spent in the country would be to have a Leaving Cert result that would be a blast! And she knew that the only way for her to achieve that would be by studying very hard. As Ebere always found chores to keep her busy at home, she decided that home was not the best place for her to study. Instead, she would go to the local library after school and on Saturdays.

Ihotu told Edache of her plans to go to the library to study in preparation for her forthcoming exams before she mentioned it to Ebere. She knew that if she told Ebere first, Ebere may not have given her approval and then, later, twist the story around to make it seem as if she was the one who didn't want to study. Edache's response to her was: "If you think that going to the library will help you concentrate better on your studies then I don't have anything against you doing that. Your results will show whether or not you actually went there to study. Make sure you get permission from your aunty before you start."

Ihotu was very happy that Edache did not object to her going to study at the library. Even though she was not totally pleased with his reply as it showed that he still did not completely trust her, but she decided not to let that bother her. Instead, she determined that she would make the most of any time that she had to spend in the library and she just hoped and prayed that Ebere would not put any obstacles in her way.

Ebere wasn't too pleased when Ihotu informed her about her study plans. "Who will prepare dinner and do the chores on Saturdays now?" she reasoned. Then she told Ihotu that she would have to discuss it with Edache first, but in her mind, however, she was trying to think of a way to stop her. As a result, she flared up when Ihotu told her that Edache had already said that she could go.

"So, why then are you coming to me about it if you and your uncle have already decided what you're going to do?" Ebere asked her angrily and walked away. Her reactions did not surprise Ihotu any longer as she had got used to them and by now could understand her very well. "Thank you, God, for delivering me from Aunty Ebere's hand this time around," Ihotu said quietly. Then with a grin, she added, "For once, I have out-smarted Aunty Ebere."

Later that day, however, Ebere confronted Edache about the issue. She said, "Honey, I thought you said Ihotu should ask me for permission about anything she wanted to do in this house."

"Yes, that's true," Edache replied.

"Then, how come you agreed her study plans with her, and even granted her permission to go to the library without me being involved?" Ebere asked.

"I did not agree anything with her," Edache responded. "She mentioned her study plans to me, and I said they were alright by me as long as she got permission from you. Did she not ask you for permission?"

Ebere explained, "Emm....she did, but to me, it seemed that she was just informing me as you had already approved her plans. You know how I am doing my best to train her to become a responsible and respectable young lady. If she continues to undermine my authority, then I will not be able to successfully achieve that goal. You can see the way her behaviour has worsened recently. If she perceives that I don't have control over her, then it is going to be very bad for all of us, especially since you are hardly ever around."

"Okay, I'm sorry," Edache said to Ebere. Then he added, "I promise not to interfere in any issue regarding Ihotu again. I hope that's alright now?"

"It's alright," Ebere said quietly.

Even though Ebere still wasn't happy and wasn't sincere about all that she had just said to Edache about Ihotu, she knew that she must never let him know her true intentions and so she decided to let the matter rest for the time being. Especially now that he had assured her again that he would not intervene in any decisions that had to do with Ihotu.

****

Leaving Cert exams were about to start. Ihotu had studied very hard as she desired to study

Accounting at university. In Ireland, admission into a desired course of study is based on passing the core subjects required for that course and also acquiring the required number of points. The points system is such that, if students score an 'A1' in a subject they acquire 100 points. An 'A2' will give them 90 points; a 'B1' will give them 85 points, and so on.

Ihotu sat for seven subjects and scored two 'A1's, three 'A2's, one 'B1' and one 'C2'. The 'C2' was in her Irish Exam, Irish being a subject she had not particularly liked. This gave her a total of 555 points as all the exams she sat were the higher level papers. It turned out that Ihotu's result was one of the three best in her school and so news of it went viral. The principal was so proud of these top three results and gave them all the publicity that he could. He did this as it served to boost the image of the school.

Ihotu had expected her uncle and his family to be excited about her results. However, she was quite taken aback when they only barely congratulated her without any form of celebrations. "Are they not happy for me? If they are, why then are they not showing it?" she wondered. In fact, Ebere did not say anything at all to her about her results. Anyway, Ihotu did not expect much praise from her after all that had been happening. "Sometimes, you can feel lonely even in the midst of people," Ihotu said to herself as she retired dejected to her room.

****

Ene, the older of Edache's two girls, was now in the second year in secondary school. She was having difficulty coping with her studies even though she was attending a private school. Edache had instructed Ihotu to assist her with her schoolwork but, even with that, there seemed to be no significant improvement in her performance. She would be going into the third year when the school resumed, which meant that she would be sitting for her Junior Cert at the end of that school year. Edache was quite concerned as he felt that Ene did not seem to be ready for this at all. Her performance had become so disappointing that he thought of arranging extra classes for her to give her more support.

Ihotu knew that Ene was quite intelligent but saw that her major challenges were being too playful and being too easily distracted. She reckoned that if Edache and Ebere could find more constructive ways to engage her and also remove major distractions from her, she would be able to concentrate better on her studies and as a result improve her performance. Ene was naturally quite a playful girl, and her mum hadn't helped the issues either. As Ihotu normally did all the housework, Ene and Ehi usually spent most of their time either watching television or playing with their toys and their numerous electronic games. Edache was hardly ever at home during the day to know how much time the girls spent on doing this and so he was unaware of how addicted to these activities they had become. Ebere, who was so good at pretending and cover-up, had a way covering up for them when their dad was home. Now Ihotu could see that Ene, who had always had it easy, would have to endure some degree of hardship if she were to pass her Junior Cert exams with good grades.

****

Is it possible to love someone and yet at the same time resent that same person? This was the question that Edache was trying to answer. Deep down inside of him, he knew that he loved Ihotu but, in the recent past, feelings of resentment towards her had also built up inside him. Could those feelings have come as a result of her excellent academic performance which tended to reveal the degree of his own children's poor performance? Or were they caused by pent-up feelings from incidents that had happened in the recent past? Being a Christian, Edache knew that harbouring feelings of resentment wasn't right and he wondered what was wrong with him to make him think like this.

He reflected on how vibrant he used to be as a Christian and said to himself, "Oh I remember those days in University, back in Nigeria, when I was on fire for the Lord! It was such a pleasant experience. Feelings like this had no place in my life. Now I know that the saying, 'Insects don't perch on a hot stove unless they want to die' is true. If it's not true that my Christian life has grown very cold, then how can all these negative feelings be so strong in my life?" Seeing how much his life had changed, he prayed silently, "Lord, have mercy on me and deliver me."

****

Two colleges offered Ihotu admission; one to study Business and the other to study Accounting. Trinity College, an old university with the reputation of being the best college in Ireland was one of them. She would have loved to go to Trinity, but her uncle said she couldn't go there because it was too expensive for him to afford the fees, and also too far from where they lived. Ihotu was not really happy with this decision and guessed that if she were his daughter, he would have been quite happy to pay for her to go there, if for no other reason, then, at least for the prestige and pride that he would enjoy when letting people know that his child was schooling at Trinity. Anyway, as they say, "beggars cannot be choosers" so she decided to obey him and take the offer from the second university. What encouraged her was the thought that if someone had told her some years back, especially following the death of her father, that one day she would be attending university in Europe, she would never have believed it. This made her grateful to God, and to think that, despite all the storms she had gone through in life, she was still making great progress.

Life in college proved very different from what she had known at secondary school. There were no longer any tutorials in the mornings, no year-head for her class, no obtaining of permission to go out of school or to come in late and so many other differences. She found it fun to have this amount of liberty but also found that with that liberty also came more responsibility. Everything just looked 'wow' and exciting to Ihotu, from the various lecture halls to the library, the canteen and, in fact, the entire college campus. Everything and everywhere seemed fabulous to her. This was her first week at university, and she had been filled with excitement all week long. As a result, she had hardly slept all week because of the thrill of it all. Several times, she had found herself imagining her future and saying to herself, "I can't believe that I am in college now. This means that, in four years, I will be a graduate and then, I will work for a big company and earn lots of money and I will be able to assist my mum, my brother, and my sister!" Thoughts like this filled her mind so much that she spent most of the nights lying awake.

Edache went to the college with her the week before lectures began to pay her fees and settle any other expenses to do with her course. On their way home he gave her a long speech on the need for her to really settle down and work hard at her studies. He finished by saying, "You are a big girl now, Ihotu. Before you are an awesome opportunity to make something great out of your life, I hope you will make me proud and not give me any reason to regret investing so much in you."

Ihotu smiled at him and responded, "Thank you so much, Uncle. I am very grateful to you for all that you have done and are still doing for me. I promise to make you very proud. You will never have any cause to regret all you have done for me."

As they continued their journey home, Edache told Ihotu interesting stories of his days in university back in Nigeria. He told her how his money and his food usually ran out before the exams started, and how he would be so broke during the exam period that he and his friends adopted a meal plan that they called 'Zero, Zero, One.' Then he explained to Ihotu how their meal plan got its name. He said, "Because of lack of funds, we had to settle for zero breakfast, zero lunch and just one dinner. That would be all the food we would have eaten each day."

Ihotu thought this was like fasting, so she asked, "Uncle, how could you fast like that during exams? How were you able to concentrate?"

He replied, "My dear, if that was a fast, then that fast was not intentional. Our financial circumstances made us live like that. As for concentrating on our books, hmmm.... we didn't have any choice if we wanted to graduate. Anyway, the human body has a way of adjusting to its' circumstances."

"Aw! I'm sorry, Uncle. It's such a pity that you had to go through all that to get through college," Ihotu said.

"Well," Edache responded, "I don't feel any pity for myself neither do I want anybody to feel pity for me. When I look back now, I could almost say, like David in the Bible that 'it was good for me that I was afflicted' because I got to where I am today as a result of what I went through back then. One can always decide to turn the pain of suffering into a passion for success," He added as they approached home.

As Ihotu opened her door to get out of the car, she thanked Edache again. She felt delighted, not just because her fees were now paid and her place in college was therefore secure but also because of the time she had spent with her uncle and the nuggets of wisdom he had given her. Thinking back, she could remember clearly that the only time she had this kind of one-to-one conversation with him was when they were on their way to Ireland almost eight years earlier. "Uncle Edache is actually a nice man. It is only when Aunty Ebere gets into the equation that things become difficult," she reasoned.

Chapter 8

Now that Ihotu was starting college, Edache felt that it would be appropriate for Ebere and him to allocate a certain amount of money each week as pocket money for her so that she didn't have to keep asking them for every little thing she needed. So he decided to have a conversation with his wife about it.

Outwardly, Ebere did not object to the idea of giving pocket money to Ihotu as her husband proposed, even though in reality she wasn't very pleased with it. As she brooded on the matter afterward, she kept asking herself. "So, this girl is actually getting out of my grip and control? What can I do to cause Edache to reverse his decision?"

Meanwhile, Ihotu was overjoyed when Edache and Ebere informed her of their decision to give her weekly pocket-money, and she thanked both of them profusely. She was so happy and felt that things were at last changing for the better between her and the two of them.

Lectures and full college activities began and, even though Ihotu found the work tough, she still enjoyed it as she loved taking on challenges. She made up her mind from day one that she was going to graduate with the highest grade possible, which would mean first class honours. She knew that no good thing comes easily and to obtain a result like that would, therefore, require a lot of hard work. It meant that she would have to attend all her lectures, study every day and do her assignments thoroughly and present them on time. She remembered some of the stories that Edache had told her of his university days back in Nigeria where some of the students were branded as '*NFA* which stood for *No Future Ambition*'. These were students who spent a lot of their time partying and hardly ever attended lectures. She wondered how they had managed to graduate, "Maybe their workload hadn't been as much as what I am facing, or they had other means of getting through," she said to herself. With the workload before her, she knew that she would not have time for any such frivolities. Anyway, partying was not her kind of lifestyle. Along with this challenging amount of schoolwork, she knew that she still would have to set time aside for helping Ebere at home with the chores. She concluded that the demands on her time was going to be very high and realised that the only way for her to succeed was to use that time very wisely.

At college, there were two other black girls, Abbey and Jane, in Ihotu's class and so, quite naturally, she became friends with them. She presumed the girls to be Christians as she recognised the names of the churches that they attended when they mentioned them. Abbey also stated that she was a member of the choir in her church. This made Ihotu happy as she felt that she had found two sisters both in the flesh and in the spirit. Everything started well, and the three of them were enthusiastic about their studies and studied together as a group. As the semester progressed, however, Ihotu began to notice some changes in the girls. At first, they talked casually about this boy or that boy, but later on, it seemed as if there was nothing else to talk about apart from boys. This made Ihotu to often draw their attention to the reason why they were in school. In response, they began to make fun of her, saying that she was 'very dry and boring'. The next change Ihotu noticed was how the girls dressed. The dresses and skirts that they wore to college could be better described as "micro" as they were far shorter than "mini." When Ihotu challenged them about this, they said that they were only dressing to match the weather, inferring that the weather was getting too warm for them. "What you are wearing would be more suited to girls going to a night-club, rather than lectures," Ihotu would scold them. But they, mocking her, would reply, "Thank you, Miss Holier than Thou."

Ihotu had her greatest shock when she discovered as time went on that the girls had started to drink alcohol and smoke cigarettes. This scared her out of her wits, and she decided that she would have a very serious talk with them about it one day after lectures.

When she eventually caught up with them, she said, "Abbey, Jane, you guys know how much I love and care about you, don't you?"

"Eehee... so what's up?" asked Abbey with a certain amount of bravado.

Ihotu continued. "There is some information that I have received, and I want to confirm if it's true. It's about both of you." Then she stopped for a moment.

"Talk *na*," said Jane breaking the silence. "Or have you suddenly become dumb or something?"

"I wonder *o*," Abbey added.

Ihotu looked straight at the two girls, plucked up courage and asked them, "Is it true that you guys have started smoking and drinking?"

"What kind of a question is that?" Abbey demanded, her eyes blazing with resentment.

Jane also reacted angrily. She asked Ihotu, "Who made you the boss over us? What right have you to be asking us a question like that?"

Ihotu could tell by their reactions that she had touched a sore point with them, so she said, "So it is true. You guys were brought up as Christians. Why have you discarded all the teachings you received from the Bible and decided to go your way? Besides all that, don't you know the damage that alcohol and cigarettes will do to your bodies? I care about you, and I'm really worried about the way you guys have decided to live your lives."

At this, the two girls got totally mad with Ihotu and walked out on her. She was stunned by their reaction as she had done what she did out of love, but unfortunately, Abbey and Jane didn't see it that way. From that point, she made up her mind to distance herself from them as she didn't want them to influence her negatively. She would still be their friend, but the friendship would not be as close as before.

Following her conversation with them, Abbey and Jane began to behave differently towards Ihotu. Whenever they passed by her, they would say something silly to each other just to get at her, but normally she just ignored what they said. Doing their best to hurt her feelings, they twisted her name and started calling her 'I-holy' instead of Ihotu. Though she found this both embarrassing and annoying, she decided to avoid saying anything back to them.

As time went on, Ihotu noticed two other girls in her class who appeared to be very serious about their studies as they were always asking intelligent questions in class and so she decided to try and make friends with them. One of them, an Irish girl, was called Orla and the other, an Asian girl, was named Anna. Although they were not Christians, Ihotu found them to be very respectful and well-mannered. She decided to join up with them anytime they had group assignments, and she liked the way they challenged her to work harder.

As the exams got closer, Abbey and Jane found that they needed Ihotu's help as the friends they had been hanging out with in the meantime hadn't much to offer at this critical time. On this particular day during the lunch break, both of them walked over to Ihotu with a smile and asked her to go to lunch with them. She politely declined, saying that she had brought lunch with her from home. She was surprised therefore to find when the girls returned, that they had brought her a pack of sandwiches and a can of soft drink.

"Ihots, we bought these for you," Jane said as she handed her the food.

Ihotu smiled to herself, noticing that they were now calling her "Ihots" rather than "I-holy." 'Ihots' was what they had fondly called her before their friendship went sour. "No, thanks!" she said. "I told you guys that I already have my lunch with me, so why did you still bother?"

"You are angry with us, and that is why you won't take the food," Abbey said to her in a bid to make her feel guilty for not taking it.

"Remember that the children of God don't hold grudges o..." Jane added, emphasising 'o' in a Nigerian accent.

"I'm not holding any grudges," Ihotu said. "Alright. To let you see that I am not angry or holding any grudge against you guys, I will take the drink." She reached into the bag with the food and took out the drink. She sensed, however, that the two of them were up to something, so she wasn't too surprised when Abbey said, "Emmm.... Ihotu, I was wondering when we can meet to revise for the exams?"

"Who is included in the 'we'?" Ihotu asked her.

"You, Abbey and I, of course!" answered Jane.

"Oh! So this is why they insisted on buying me lunch," Ihotu thought as she wryly smiled to herself. However, she decided to help them still because she wanted them to perform well in their exams, and so she asked them reluctantly, "What time is convenient for you guys?"

"We will work along with whatever suits your schedule," they said, answering her simultaneously.

Ihotu knew that meeting up with Abbey and Jane to revise would more than likely turn out to be her doing most of the work as they hadn't been taking their studies seriously ever since the beginning of the semester. She didn't mind too much because she reckoned that if she were imparting knowledge to them, then she would be getting a better understanding of her coursework. She told them that she could meet with them on two occasions before the exams which were to commence the following week. They were pleased with the arrangement, and they agreed on the time and place to meet. However, by the end of the second session,

Abbey and Jane realised that they still needed more help.

Jane turned to Ihotu and asked, "Can we meet again on Saturday for some extra study?"

"Yeah, I agree. Let's meet on Saturday," Abbey added.

Ihotu, seeing that this would create problems for her was quiet for a moment. Then she said, "I'm sorry, guys. I wish we could have more time to study together, but I have to help at home on Saturdays. Any remaining time after that, I will have to use for my revision."

"Okay," Abbey and Jane responded as if pleased with Ihotu's explanation, but they were not happy. When Ihotu left, Abbey looked at Jane and said, "You can see now how big Ihotu feels about herself, can't you?"

"It's not her fault. How will she not feel big when she knows that we now need her help?" Jane asked as both of them got ready to leave as well.

****

The semester's exams came and went. When the results were released, Ihotu found that she had done very well in each of her five modules while Abbey had passed only three modules and failed two and Jane, on the other hand, had passed four. Neither of them was pleased with their results and felt that it was Ihotu's fault that they had failed some of their modules.

"If we had had that Saturday session with Ihotu that we requested, I'm sure we would have passed all our modules," said Jane to Abbey as they looked over their results.

"That's true," Abbey agreed with her. She thought about it for a while and then said, "Ihotu thinks she is the only clever girl on this campus. I think we should teach her a lesson."

"You're right," Jane responded, nodding her head. Then she added, "She needs to know that passing exams is not the only measure of smartness. We will show her that we are much smarter than she is."

In full agreement with each other, they started planning on how best to get at Ihotu. Before long, they came up with the idea of breaking into her personal email account and then send emails to people using content that would implicate her and put her in a bad light. The immediate challenge confronting them was how to get hold of her password.

Then Jane thought of one possibility. "I think I know her student account password," she said. "Remember the day when she asked me to help her submit her Financial Management assignment because she had received an urgent call from her aunt and had to rush home? You know she wanted to submit her work on the portal before leaving but, because I hadn't quite finished, I told her I needed hers as a guide to help me to finish mine, so she gave me her password and asked me to submit it for her when I was through."

"Then let's try the password you have on her Yahoo email account. You know, a lot of people use the same password for most of their online activities," said Abbey with a glint in her eye.

Quickly, they hurried to the school library, logged on to a computer, and proceeded to Yahoo Mail. Lo and behold, when they entered Ihotu's username and the password that Abbey had, they found that the email account opened! "Yeah..... it worked!" they exclaimed excitedly as they both high-fived each other in celebration of their success in this first phase of their plan. The stern look from another student sitting close by made them realise that they were in the library where noise was not tolerated. They quickly quietened down and proceeded to send the first email now that the way was open.

This email was written to Steve, a student in their class, whom they knew was interested in Ihotu. Pretending to be Ihotu, they giggled in anticipation as Abbey made suggestions and Jane typed the message which read as follows:

"Dear Steve,

I'm really sorry for the way I treated you the other day. I have come to realise that you are a very cool guy and I want us to meet up soon so that I can show you how much you mean to me.

XoXoXo,

Ihotu."

They took turns to read over the short email, nodded to each other, and Jane pressed the 'send' key.

As soon as Steve read the email, he was stunned. He thought, "What on earth is going on? Does this mean Ihots has fallen for me after all? This is too good to be true!" He decided to reply using Facebook Messenger to say that they could meet the next day after lectures. He felt that this would be a faster way to get her attention instead of replying by email.

When Ihotu saw his Facebook message, she was more than a little surprised but paid no attention to it. She reasoned, "I thought he had stopped all this. I can't believe that he is still asking to meet up with me. Maybe, if I continue to ignore him, he will eventually give up and leave me alone."

The next day at college, Steve made sure that he sat near Ihotu in class. His face was beaming and, seeing him so cheery, Ihotu wondered what was up with him. Suddenly, he leaned towards her and whispered, "I'm really happy to know that you want to meet up with me. Can we get together this evening?"

Ihotu, still unsure of what exactly was up with him, answered, "Who wants to meet with you? You must be kidding, right? Steve, I want to concentrate on my work today so, if you don't mind, please excuse me." At this, she picked up her books, took her bag, and moved to sit at the other end of the room.

Abbey and Jane, who were sitting right behind them, began to snigger. Steve, embarrassed, glanced at them and strode out of the lecture-room. They followed him and called him over to a corner where they asked to have a talk with him.

Jane started the conversation. "Steve," she said, "we're really sorry for the embarrassment that Ihotu caused you just now. You know she is our friend and whatever she does affects us too. Actually, she likes you and she's only playing hard to get."

"Yes, she really likes you, but I don't know what her problem is. If you cooperate with us, we will make sure that she becomes yours very soon," Abbey added.

Steve, who all the while had been trying to control his anger, blurted out, "Can you imagine her sending me an email asking when we can meet up and then start this drama as soon as she sees me? What the hell is the matter with her?"

Jane answered with a soothing voice, "Take it easy, Steve. Everything is going to be alright. Just listen to what we tell you."

Steve, completely taken in by their pretence, replied, "Yeah, just tell me, what is it you want me to do? I am ready to do anything to get Ihots."

Abbey, jotting down her email address for him, told him what to do: "The next time you get an email from her, forward it to me at this address. Just continue to be nice to her. Jane and I will put pressure on her from our end to make her give in to you."

From where they stood talking, they could see Mr. Fisher, the lecturer for their next class, entering the lecture room, so they quickly ended their conversation and dashed back to their seats. At the end of lectures that day, as Abbey and Jane walked to catch their buses home, they had a good laugh when they remembered the incidents of the day and the embarrassment they had caused both Ihotu and Steve.

"I think we should act fast before Ihotu notices that her email account has been hacked into and changes her password," Abbey said.

"Yeah, you're right," said Jane. "So, what do you have in mind?" She could see from the look on Abbey's face that she had thought of something really clever.

"I think this time, we should send not one but two sweet emails from Ihotu's email account, one to Steve, thanking him for their time together and apologising for her behaviour in class. The other one will be to someone called Kunle, a fake email account that we will set up," said Abbey gleefully.

"Your brain is like a razor blade! See how sharp it is! How I wish it were just as sharp when you're faced with your college work," Jane said jokingly, as she smiled and nodded in agreement with Abbey's idea.

With that, they decided to go back to the School Library and use the computers there to carry out this self-imposed assignment before going home. While there, Abbey created a 'Kunle Ade' fake email account while Jane worded the emails they were planning to send. In the email that they sent to Steve, they made it appear as if Steve was

Ihotu's boyfriend whom she met with secretly but did not want to be seen publicly. On the other hand, the email they sent to Kunle made it look like he was another boyfriend that Ihotu had, who kept the money he made from *'deals'* with her, and she was at liberty to spend some of the money. Abbey and Jane felt so satisfied after this assignment as they logged out of the system to go home.

"We'll watch and see how our *'Miss I-Holy'* will get herself out of this one by the time her guardians get to read these emails," Jane said to Abbey as they headed for the bus-stop.

Chapter 9

The second semester was progressing well for Ihotu. She had been doing a lot of additional studies with Anna and Orla and was happy with her performance so far. She was even happier because things were also going well between her and her uncle's family. There hadn't been any serious issue with Ebere, and she was thankful for that. The semester exams were just a few weeks away, and she was determined to work very hard to improve on her first semester results. Although those results had been very good, she still felt she could do better this time. "After all, I didn't score a hundred percent in any of my modules, so that means there is room for improvement," she said to herself.

One evening, while in the library after the day's lectures, Ihotu checked her phone and was surprised to find that she had missed seven calls. Her phone had been on 'silent' because of the 'no-noise' policy in the library. When she looked to see who had been calling, she discovered that the missed calls were from her mum in Nigeria. At this, she became alarmed because she thought, "Why would mummy have called me so many times? Oh, Lord, I hope everything is okay." Quickly, she walked outside to return the call. Being able to make the call made her grateful, and as she made the connection, she said to herself, "Thank God for this allowance that I am getting. At least I have enough credit on my phone to make and return urgent calls like this one. God bless Uncle Edache and Aunty Ebere for doing this for me!"

Her younger brother, Agada, was the one who answered the phone. "How are you, Agada? Where is mummy?" Ihotu asked impatiently before Agada could even reply to her first question. The line was quiet for a while as Agada said nothing. "Are you still there? Can you hear me?" she asked again.

"Yes, I can hear you," Agada replied. "Mummy is in hospital. She collapsed this morning and had to be rushed to the hospital. We don't know yet what is wrong with her as the doctors are still carrying out tests."

Agada sounded upset, so Ihotu tried to say something encouraging to him. "Mum will be fine, just be strong, I will ring back later, but if you hear the results before then, you just call me. Okay?"

"Okay," said Agada.

When Ihotu hung up, the tears that had welled up in her eyes flowed down her face. She had tried to be strong when speaking to Agada because she wanted to sound encouraging as she could only imagine what he and Precious, her little sister, were going through at this time. "Dear Lord, don't let anything be seriously wrong with Mummy. She has suffered enough hardship. Please make her healthy again so that she can enjoy the fruit of her labours. Lord, please intervene!" She prayed aloud, with the tears still flowing freely but, when she remembered that she was in a public place, she quickly wiped her eyes so as not to draw attention to herself. Aware that she might be looking awful, she went to the bathroom where she washed and dried her face and tried to freshen her make-up before heading back to the library. However, she realised that she could no longer concentrate on her studies, so she just packed her books and headed for home.

When she got there, she discovered that Edache had already been informed about her mother taking ill. He explained, "After work today, I saw several missed calls from your mum on my phone. When I rang back, I discovered that it was Agada that had been calling, and he then told me about what had happened to your mum." After a pause, he added, "Anyway, let's be hopeful. Maybe she collapsed due to stress. You know how hard she works. I'm sure the hospital staff will know how best to help her."

"Uncle, I just hope so," said Ihotu, "I really hope so."

Early the following morning, Ihotu decided to ring Agada again to find out how things were and to inquire if the doctors had said anything about what might be wrong with their mum. In answer to her questions, Agada said, "Mummy has been on one drip after another since she was brought to the hospital yesterday, and she has been sleeping most of the time." Then he added, "Precious and I are okay, and Aunty Onma is staying with us for the time being. The only thing the doctors have said to us is that Mum's blood-count is very low and that they are still investigating the cause of this."

Ihotu, hearing that her siblings were not alone at a time like this, felt happy about that. She asked to speak to Onma, and when she answered, she thanked her for her support. She also spoke to Precious who kept crying on the phone and asking her when she was coming back home. As she sobbed, she kept pleading, "Please come back home, Ihotu. I'm missing you." Ihotu's heart broke when she heard Precious cry and plead with her to come home.

"Doesn't she realise that if I had my way, I would be back home with them and be by Mum's side ever since I heard the news?" Ihotu thought quietly. She decided to assure Precious that she was missing her very much too, and the rest of her family as well. Then she explained how it wasn't possible for her to come home just yet.

When Ihotu ended the call, tears rolled down her cheeks. "Oh, Lord, when will I ever stop crying? Please intervene in this situation and bring my mother out of the hospital," she said, crying and praying at the same. It took a lot of effort for her to pull herself together and get ready for college because she felt so downcast, but she needed to go because her exams were only a few weeks away. "If I had my way, I would not get out of bed today!" she said to herself, "but I cannot afford such luxury. Daddy, please help me and give me the strength to do all that is required of me today," she prayed to her heavenly Father as she pulled herself out of bed.

It was during her lunch break that Ihotu discovered that God hears the little prayers that we whisper during our low moments. Somehow, she had managed to do all that was required of her up to that point in the day. She did her chores before leaving home, attended her lectures, and had also done a bit of studying. It was when she went out to have her lunch that Agada rang. Having been expecting that call all day, she jumped at it.

"Yes, Agada, any news?" she enquired of her brother.

"Hmmm…….." Agada sighed heavily.

"What is it, Agada? Can you hear me?" Ihotu asked, getting impatient.

"Ihotu, it's not good news," said Agada slowly. "The doctors told us that Mum has leukaemia! They said it is…"

Before he could say another word, Ihotu screamed, "Leukae… what? It's not true! Mummy just cannot have leukaemia. No, no, no…." she found herself screaming the words over and over as she ended the call. She only realised that she had drawn attention to herself when another student came to ask her if she was okay. "It's just some bad news from home. I'm sorry for disturbing you," she said to him. Then, she carried her bag and went to look for a quiet place where she could cry without disturbing anyone else.

She found an empty lecture room, went inside, and closed the door behind herself. She sat down, put her head on the table, and burst into tears. She found herself weeping and praying at the same time. She kept on saying, "God, this is one battle that you must win for us. My mummy cannot die just yet. That is why she must not have leukaemia. No, Lord, I refuse to accept this report. You have to intervene and change the situation." She didn't know how long she spent in that room, but she must have been there for hours. It was only when the janitor came to lock up for the night that she became aware of where she was. She couldn't believe that it was evening already! She had to leave immediately and make her way home.

She went straight to her room as soon as she got home. She didn't have the strength for any pleasantries or even to eat her dinner. She had cried so much during the day that she wasn't able to cry anymore. She laid on her bed, staring at the wall with many different thoughts racing through her mind. Suddenly, she got an idea. She would make a deal with the Lord! "Yes, that's it!" She said aloud. Then she went ahead and loudly made this promise to God, "Lord, if you will heal my mother completely of this leukaemia, I promise to dedicate the rest of my life to you. I will serve you and tell people of what you have done anywhere I get a chance in this whole wide world."

In the church, she had been taught the power of making a covenant with God, an agreement where a person vows, "Lord if you will do this for me, I, in turn, will do that for you." She clearly remembered the story of Hannah in the Bible. For several years, Hannah had hoped for a child but wasn't able to have one. Then she made a covenant with God, saying that if God gave her a male child, she would dedicate him to the Lord. Ihotu also remembered how the story said that God answered Hannah's prayer speedily. She also recalled how her pastor would say humorously, that God answered her in a hurry because 'God is a God of deals.' The deal, as the pastor explained, was that God needed a new priest to lead His people as the current priest, Eli was old, and his time in office was almost over. God was angry with Eli's sons and refused to allow them to take over from their father. This was why God was pleased with the deal that Hannah proposed - *'Give me a son, and I'll give you a priest!'* The deal suited both of them, and that was why God answered her prayer immediately.

With the memory of the story of Hannah and the agreement with the Lord that Ihotu had just entered, she felt a sense of inner peace. Somehow, something deep down her heart told her that God had heard her request and that He was going to heal her mum completely. With that assurance, she resolved in her heart to keep her part of the deal.

She knew that leukaemia was a kind of cancer and so could be fatal. During a Cancer Awareness week, back in her sixth year in secondary school, people from the Cancer Society of Ireland had come to her school to enlighten the students about the different types of cancer. They had also discussed ways that the students could support their work by spreading awareness in order to raise funds for the Society. Leukaemia had been one of the types of cancer that they were told about. She recalled some of the girls volunteering to shave off their hair as a way of raising funds for the Society and support for people living with cancer. That was the reason why she couldn't let Agada finish talking when he was trying to explain to her what leukaemia was. Now that she felt a bit better, thoughts of Agada and Precious flooded into her mind, and she admitted to herself, "Only God knows what they are going through right now, especially after the way I reacted this afternoon when Agada broke the news to me. I must ring them later tonight and encourage them," she said as she pulled herself out of bed and went downstairs.

When she got there, she found Edache sitting in the living room with Ebere, and she greeted them. From their reactions, it was obvious that they had received news of her mother's condition.

"Oh, Ihotu, there you are. Come here to me," said Ebere. As Ihotu moved closer, Ebere got up and put her arm around her shoulders and brought her to sit beside her. "Your uncle has just told me about your mum. I was about to come upstairs to your room just before you came downstairs. I know it must be very hard for you right now," she said as she pulled Ihotu close to her.

Ihotu couldn't believe what she was seeing and hearing. "Can Aunty Ebere actually be as compassionate as?" she queried in her mind. "Is she really sincere in what she is doing right now, or is she doing one of her pretentious acts? Anyway, whatever it is, it feels good to have someone to lean on right now," Ihotu concluded.

Then Edache spoke up, trying to say something encouraging. "Ihotu, leukaemia does not kill people instantly. With treatment, your mum stands a good chance of being cured. Let us be positive and hopeful that she will be one of the people who survive this illness."

However, his words did little to console Ihotu. She said, "Thank you, Uncle. Thank you, Aunty. I really want to believe God for a miracle because my mum just cannot die right now." Then she burst into tears again.

"She is not going to die," said Ebere in her attempt to console Ihotu.

"Your aunty and I will do whatever we can to support your mum at this difficult time," said Edache trying to reassure Ihotu.

"Go and get yourself something to eat," said Ebere. "I noticed that you didn't eat anything since you came back from school this evening."

Ihotu thanked them again as she stood up to go to the kitchen. She had actually not eaten anything all day. She didn't have any breakfast before she left home that morning, and it was just before her lunch that she received the devastating news of her mum's terrible illness.

Chapter 10

Her doctors listed prescriptions and procedures necessary for Ahubi's treatment, and it was apparent that hundreds of thousands of Nigerian naira would be required for her treatment. Ihotu was surprised by the generous donations that came from family and friends. Edache also sent a substantial amount of money towards the cost of the treatment. "Thank God for kind-hearted people," Ihotu said to herself as she saw the way many people were going out of their way to support her mum. To her, it was the first sign that God wanted her mum to live.

With the commencement of her treatment, Ahubi's health began to improve. She was diagnosed with Acute Myeloid Leukaemia (AML), which was said to worsen very rapidly if treatment wasn't commenced immediately after it was detected. She was told that her treatment would be in two stages; the first round of treatment would be an induction therapy aiming to achieve remission by killing as many AML cells as possible. This should return her blood count to normal over time and get rid of any signs of the disease for a long period. Her treatment would also include blood transfusions, chemotherapy, and various other things. Ihotu was very thankful to God as her mum began to respond to treatment and, each time she spoke with her brother and sister, she always encouraged them to have an attitude of gratitude to God, thanking Him in advance for their mum's full recovery. She had been taught that faith meant being confident that what you hoped for would happen. Therefore, she chose to thank God in this way because she believed that her mum would recover her full health.

After several weeks in the hospital, Ahubi was discharged. She was making good progress, and her health seemed to have returned to normal. She was given an appointment for a check-up after a couple of weeks at home, after which the consolidation therapy, which was the second round of treatment, would be scheduled. By this time, Ihotu was full of gratitude to God, believing that God had completely healed her mother. She did not hesitate to say this to the people in her church and to anyone else who cared to listen.

In the meantime, the second-semester exams had come and gone. Ihotu didn't find them easy at all as they were held during the period that her mum was in the hospital. She did her best to concentrate on her studies, but it was so easy for her mind to wander to thoughts of her mum and the situation at home instead of focussing on her work. Anyway, she was happy enough that she was still able to do them. It was good that she had worked hard right from the beginning of the semester and she found that, when she couldn't work as hard as she wanted during the exams, she had a lot of residual knowledge to fall back on. When the results were released, she was pleasantly surprised to find that she had passed each of her exams and passed them well! Now the way was open for her to progress to the second year.

****

"Ihotu!" Edache called out in a deep, solemn voice. Ihotu rushed to the living room and found Edache sitting there with Ebere. He had some papers in his hand. At first, she thought they might be documents to do with college but wondered why they would send her correspondence to him as they normally corresponded with her directly. As moved closer and looked at Edache's face, it dawned on her that something unpleasant was about to happen.

"Sit down!" Edache orderly sharply, the tone of his voice confirming her feelings that all was not well. As soon as she did, Edache handed her the papers and asked her to explain the meaning of what was written on them. She looked at the first one trying to make sense of it when she discovered that it was an email sent from her email address. On a closer look, she found that it was an email that she had purportedly sent to Steve.

She was so shocked that she gasped, "Ah! What is this? I don't understand any of it."

"You don't understand what?" Edache barked at her. Then he continued, his voice filled with anger, "You don't understand the emails you send to your boyfriends anymore? Honestly, Ihotu, you never cease to amaze me. Just when I am beginning to regain confidence in you, you ruin it all again."

Then Ebere joined in the conversation. She tried to offer some explanation about how the emails got to them. "In case you are wondering how those emails got to us, your friends Abbey and Jane forwarded them to me," she said. "You can see that this one sent to Steve was forwarded to Abbey, who then forwarded it to me. And the one sent to this other boy called Kunle was forwarded directly from his account to me, as you can see."

Ihotu, reeling from the shock of this apparent disaster, spoke with a stammer as she tried to explain. "Honestly, Uncle, Aunty, believe me, I don't know what this is all about; it must be some kind of scam. Yes, Steve is in the same class as I am, but I have never in my life sent him an email, and I don't even know who this Kunle Ade is."

Ebere who wasn't interested in any explanation that Ihotu had to make, sneered at her. "How come what you call a 'scam' only involves two boys and no other person on your contact list?" She continued, "We notice that you have been sending money home to Nigeria, the money you are getting from Kunle."

Ihotu, still trying to sort out in her mind what was happening, offered her best explanation. "It was just once I sent fifty euro to Agada. That was when mummy was initially taken into hospital, and he had told me that he hadn't eaten anything all that day because there was no food in the house. This happened before mummy's diagnosis and before you, and other people contributed money to help pay for her treatment. The money I sent was all that I had managed to save out of the weekly pocket-money you give me. I always try to save some, no matter how little, each time you gave me pocket money."

Ebere wasn't at all convinced. So, she asked, "After you pay for your weekly travel pass out of the money that we give you, you barely have ten euro left. Now you want us to believe that ten euro is enough to keep you for a week and even allow you to save some out of it?"

"Yes," said Ihotu, wondering where all these questions were taking her. Then she added, "I try to save at least five euro every week as I hardly buy anything in college, and I always make sure that I take lunch with me from home."

Ebere interrupted her, still not convinced. She said, "Ihotu, I seriously think that it is you who is the 'scam' here. Recently, I noticed you were wearing new clothes which I didn't buy for you and I wondered how you were able to afford them. Now I know. It is quite obvious that you have another source of income."

"Aunty, it's only two dresses that I bought during the whole session, and I bought them at the local charity shop. You know how one can sometimes be fortunate to find new clothes there," explained Ihotu, denying Ebere's allegation.

"Enough of this nonsense!" Edache interrupted with a stern voice. "Honestly, I am completely disappointed with you, Ihotu. Your explanations don't carry any weight as far as I can see. Get out of here now before I lose my temper altogether. When I decide what to do about your behaviour, I will let you know. Now off with you!"

Ihotu walked out of the room with her head bowed. As soon as she was out of earshot, Ebere turned to Edache and said, "Sweetheart, you had better think seriously about this, because I'm not sure whether the money you are spending on this girl is an investment or a waste. If this is the kind of thing she is getting involved in, then I wonder if she will eventually graduate at all. Remember, our children are growing up very fast and will soon be entering college as well."

Ihotu shut herself into her room, still holding the two emails in her hand. She sat down on the edge of her bed and looked at them, reading them over and over again to herself. The first one, the one she was supposed to have sent to Steve, read:

"Hey Sweetie,
Thanks for last nite. It's always great fun hanging out with you. You are so sweet, and I can't imagine life without you. Baby, thoughts of you and the memory of the beautiful time

we spent together stole away my sleep. Can't wait to see you in college on Monday!

Chat later Snapchat. Have to do some chores now. Love you lots!

XoXoXo,
Ihots."

The second email, the one supposedly sent to this person called Kunle, read as follows:

"Hey Baby,
What's up? Why aren't you picking up your fone? You still mad at me, eh?
I'm sorry! Ok! You know I can't live without you, so please don't keep me in the dark. Call me and let's talk it over. About the money, it's not that I don't appreciate how you allow me spend some of it. As you know, the holidays are approaching, and I always have to be home, and so it will be very difficult for me to continue to keep it. My aunty may get aware of it, and you know what that would mean for me.

Thanks for all your support. I wonder how miserable my life would have been without you. Please ring me, and we'll arrange to meet up soon. Otherwise, I will transfer the money to Naija o, lol....just kidding.
Love you lots.
Ihots."

Ihotu read over the two emails several more times, but she could still not make any sense out of either of them. As she thought about them, she began to wonder. "Both emails are dated May, and this is now August. How come they are only coming to Uncle and Aunty now?" As she considered the style of the wording, she reasoned, "Anyone who ever received an email from me would know that this is not my style of writing. And the worst of it all is the fact that I don't even know anyone by the name of Kunle Ade! It is obvious to me that I have been scammed, but the saddest thing for me is that Uncle and Aunty will not believe my explanations! Why are they always so suspicious of me? Why are they always choosing to believe the worst instead of the best about me?" Then she prayed, "God, only you can deliver me from allegations like these as there is nothing I can say that will make them believe me."

While she sat there, going over the content of the emails, her phone rang. It was her mum. Ihotu was so happy to hear from her, especially as she sounded very excited. Ahubi told Ihotu that she went for a check-up that very morning and the doctors told her that she had achieved remission and her blood count was now normal. "This is proof," she added, "that I am doing really well."

"Oh, praise God!" was all Ihotu could say. She was already up on her feet before her mum could even finish speaking. She had momentarily forgotten her own problems as she joined with her mum in rejoicing with the good news.

Wanting to know all the details, Ihotu asked her mum, "So what did the doctors say you should do now?"

"They said I should continue taking my medicines and make an appointment to go in for the consolidation therapy. This is the second round of treatment that I need to destroy any remaining leukaemia cells and prevent a re-occurrence of the disease," Ahubi replied.

"So, have you made that appointment?" Ihotu asked.

Ahubi hesitated before she answered, "Hmm..... My daughter, making that appointment depends on me having the money to pay for it. They told me that the consolidation therapy was quite expensive, about the same as what I spent on the first stage of my treatment." She paused again. Then she said to Ihotu, "Where on earth am I going to get such a huge amount of money, Ihotu? Honestly, I don't know what to do."

Ihotu, remembering how God had stepped in and helped her when she needed money, encouraged her mum, "Mummy, let's continue to trust God to supply all that you need. So far, He has proved faithful just as the Bible says He is. I believe that He can finish what He has started."

Ahubi was really impressed by her daughter's faith and by her knowledge of the Bible, and it gave her great encouragement listening to her talk like this. The little girl that she used to tell Bible stories to was now the person teaching her. She found herself smiling as she said to Ihotu, "Yes, it's true Ihotu! God is able to complete what He has started, and I believe He will perfect my healing." As she ended the call, she whispered to Ihotu, "Baby-girl, I'm so proud of you!"

Ihotu's countenance brightened as her mum spoke those words. She remarked to herself, "It's as if mum exactly knew what I needed to hear right now! She said, 'I'm so proud of you.' Oh, how I desperately needed to hear those words! Uncle Edache told me just a little while ago how disappointed he is with me, and now my mum phones and says she is proud of me. Which of these two people will I believe?" Ihotu knew the answer to her question, and so she said, "My mum, of course! She knows me best. She trusts me, and she believes the best about me."

Ihotu realised that the conversation with her mum had given her the strength that she needed. It would last for the moment, at least.

Chapter 11

Following the talk that Edache and Ebere had with Ihotu about the two emails, things had not remained the same between them and her, and she found that living with them seemed like living with two strangers. Neither of them hardly said anything to her anymore, and the only words shared between them were brief hellos and goodbyes. She also noticed that Ene and Ehi were behaving funnily toward her. As she hated suspense, she wondered, "Whatever they have in mind, why don't they just tell me?"

Eventually, Ihotu plucked-up courage and managed to remind her uncle a week before school resumed, about the opening date and her fees.

"Is that so?" was all the reply that he gave her, and this made her even more confused. "What does he mean by answering me like that?" she wondered.

However, when college eventually resumed, she went to him on the morning of the first day to remind him again, and without saying anything, he handed her fifty euro. She was a bit confused by this as she didn't know if the money was for her weekly pocket-money or for something else as the money was more than the weekly allowance that he normally gave her. She waited for a while as she expected him to say something, but he still said nothing. She opened her mouth to ask him about the money, but the look on his face frightened her, so she kept quiet. Instead, she just thanked him and left for college. She did whatever part of her registration that she could, but she felt very restricted because she had not paid her fees.

Classes were scheduled to commence straightway. On the very first day, Ihotu met Abbey and Jane, and she was quite taken aback because, when they saw her, instead of the usual pleasantries that they would normally exchange after not seeing one another for a while, they both looked at each other and giggled. Ihotu felt embarrassed by their attitude, and so she just said, 'Hi' to them and walked away. She knew she needed to have a serious talk with them sometime soon, but she also knew that she needed to keep her emotions under control so that they couldn't make her react in a bad way. She hoped that when she got the chance, they would be cooperative and not make things even more difficult.

And so, a few days later, after things had settled down and college activities were becoming pretty normal, Ihotu decided to call Abbey and Jane aside to talk with them about what had been happening.

"Thanks for coming," said Ihotu, opening the conversation. "I notice that things have not been going very smoothly between us, and I want to know if there is anything I have done that you are not happy about?"

"So, is that why you called us here? To interrogate us?" said Abbey immediately flaring up.

Jane, also spoke defiantly, "You are too full of yourself, Ihotu. Imagine summoning us for interrogation like this."

Ihotu tried her best to calm the two girls down. Holding up her hands, she said, "Okay, guys, I'm sorry if the way my words came out seemed offensive to you, but I didn't mean it like that. I'm just concerned about the way things are between us."

Jane was still defiant. She said, "The only problem I have with you; Ihotu is that you are too full of yourself."

Ihotu was puzzled by this statement, so she asked, "How? In what way am I full of myself?"

"Maybe it's because you think you are the only intelligent and clever girl in this college," Abbey added.

Her words made Ihotu even more amazed, so she said, "But you guys have never said anything like this to me before. In fact, you used to tell me that I was very humble. So how then did I suddenly get filled with myself?"

Jane, agreeing with Abbey, blurted out, "You think you are more intelligent than us. And you also feel that you are now better than us, isn't it?"

"Can you even imagine the 'shakara' (Nigerian slang used in this context for being snobbish or conceited) you did for us when we requested that we study together?" said Abbey.

At that, Ihotu began to understand the reason for their harshness. She remembered the day they wanted her help, but she had been too busy to give them any more of her time. So, she responded, "Ah! You mean you guys are still holding that against me? That incident happened close to a year ago. Remember, it was just before our first semester exams in the first year. You know I wasn't doing *shakara*. I explained to you at the time why I couldn't make that Saturday session that you requested."

Jane spoke, her voice now a little softer, "Anyway, you can see that even without your help, we still passed our second-semester exams."

Ihotu was quick to take advantage of her change of tone. She looked straight at her and said, "There! That proves it! You don't need me to pass your exams *na*. Am I God? Or am I the lecturer marking your papers? Look, guys, I am happy for both of you that you made it through. That is what I want for each of us that we make progress together. I apologise for any misunderstanding that my words or actions may have caused. Please let's put the past behind us and be friends again."

However, Abbey and Jane just shrugged their shoulders, and that was all the response Ihotu got from them. So, after a brief silence, she asked them: "My aunty showed me some emails, and she said it was you guys who sent them to her."

Jane was immediately defensive. "And so?" she retorted.

Ihotu held her ground and continued with her questions. "But why would you guys do a thing like that? Anyway, how did you even come across those emails?"

Now it was Abbey's turn to be vehement. With a sneer, she said, "Well, Miss Pretender, we explained to your aunt how we got them. Did she not tell you?"

At this, Ihotu could hardly hold back her tears. She looked at the two girls and said, "Honestly, I didn't send either of those emails. And if you were my friends, when you saw such things involving me, why didn't you ask me about them first?"

"Let's go," said Abbey to Jane. "Now that her secrets have got out into the open, she wants to blame us for what she has done."

At this, they both walked out on Ihotu. She just stood there wide-eyed, really astonished by their behaviour. Then she sat down, and for a while, she was asking herself so many questions that gave her reasons to re-evaluate her relationship with these two girls who she had thought were her friends. "Are Abbey and Jane really my friends? Do they care about me the way I care about them? Why do they seem so unbothered by their actions which are almost destroying my life?" Then she concluded, "It is obvious that they are up to something and there may be many more things that I don't know yet. But as the saying goes: 'Whatever interrogation cannot reveal, time will reveal.' I will wait and see. I'm sure that with time, a lot of things will become clearer." With this assurance, she stood up to go home.

****

It was now five weeks since college resumed and Edache still had not paid Ihotu's fees neither had he said anything at all to her about them. The small amount of money that he gave her, occasionally, was what she had been using to pay for her transport each day. "Has he got tired of sponsoring me? Is he having financial difficulties? Oh, why doesn't he just say something?" Ihotu found herself musing after Edache handed her twenty euro that morning when she was ready to leave for college. "Maybe, I need to remind him again," she reasoned to herself.

That evening, she got another shock when Edache called her in for another talk. He told her how enormous his responsibilities were and how they were becoming more than he could cope with. He mentioned how her mother had phoned him, asking for help again to pay for another round of treatment. He said his girls were getting to the age when they would soon be ready to go to college but, his extended family responsibilities would not allow him to save enough to cater for their future adequately. He informed her that sponsoring her in college was a huge sacrifice for him to make, and now her recent shameful acts had caused him to re-think his commitment. He concluded by saying that he would no longer be able to support her by paying her college fees. There was no 'maybe' in his words. His mind seemed made-up.

Ihotu was speechless. Immediately, all sorts of questions came into her mind, "Did I hear him correctly? So, what does he want me to do now? Where does he expect me to go from here? Why did he allow me to start college if he knew that he was not going to sponsor me all the way through?"

As Ihotu wasn't saying anything, Edache continued, "You know you are over eighteen years of age now. That makes you an adult according to the laws of this country. You could go and get a job and change your course to a part-time one. Alternatively, you could work full-time for a while and save up enough money to pay for your college fees."

Ihotu still was very quiet. She couldn't believe what she had just heard from her uncle. Ever since her senior years in secondary school, she had wanted to work part-time during the holidays to support Edache, but he had never allowed her. Ebere had also been against the idea because if she went to work, it would mean that she would no longer be available to do the house chores. Even during the summer holidays just gone, she had desperately wanted to work, but they still didn't allow her.

When Edache finished his speech, he stood up and left the living room. Ihotu sat there, too confused and shocked even to think. It was only after a little while when she got up and went to her room, that she flung herself on to her bed and burst into tears. "How will I survive this? Oh, God, where do I go from here?" She kept saying these things over and over to herself as she wept. Lying there, memories of her dad flashed before her, and she began to moan: "Daddy, where are you? Can't you see what I'm going through? Why did you leave me so early? Why was death so cruel as to take you away from me?"

Ihotu must have cried herself to sleep because she woke up late in the night to discover that she was sleeping in the same clothes that she had worn to college in the morning. She got up, changed into her night clothes, and went back to bed but found that she could no longer sleep. Instead, she could think a little more clearly now about her situation than when her uncle was speaking to her. After some serious thought, she resolved that she was not going to drop out of college unless they should somehow bundle her up and throw her out. She also decided that she was going to look for a part-time job that would suit the hours that she spent at college.

The next day, while sitting alone during her lunch-break, she got a call from Agada. She had been thinking about her family for about two days now and had wanted to ring them the day before, but then the meeting with Edache changed everything. She was happy to hear her brother's voice as she hoped that a call from home would cheer her up. She recalled the last time she spoke with her mum and the encouraging words she had said to her.

"Hello Agada, how are you?" said Ihotu to her brother.

"I'm good, Sis," he replied.

"How are Mummy and Precious?" Ihotu asked.

"Precious is okay," Agada replied.

"And mum?" Ihotu asked with a certain feeling of apprehension.

"Actually, that is why I am calling you. Mum is not feeling very well at the moment. It looks as if the symptoms of leukaemia are starting to show up in her again," Agada replied.

Ihotu was silent as she tried to take in this bad news. So much so that Agada had to ask, "Ihotu, can you hear me?"

After a moment or two, Ihotu responded, her voice very quiet, "Hmm...... I can hear you, Agada. But what is the meaning of all that's going on? Why are all these bad things happening to us?" She realised she couldn't continue the conversation any further and so she said, "Agada, please give me some time, I will call you back later." Then she hung up.

With this terrible news, Ihotu became completely weak, too weak even to cry. She just sat there with her eyes wide open like someone who has lost her mind. After a long time, she said to herself, "These problems are more than I can bear. I need help, but where will I get that help? I need someone to talk to, but who can I trust? In whom can I confide? Will I go to the pastor of our church and talk with him? No! Uncle Edache and Aunty Ebere are part of his leadership team, and there is no way that I can tell him about all that I am going through without implicating them. Moreover, would he even believe me?"

She sat there, lost in these her conflicting thoughts when she became aware that someone was talking to her. "I have been watching you for a while. It seems to me that you are very troubled." It was a young man who introduced himself to her, giving his name as Patrick.

Ihotu looked up at him, trying to make sense of what he was saying to her. He repeated what he had said and told her that he had said 'hello' to her about three times before he managed to get her attention.

"Yes, I am troubled," she answered, "but it's about personal matters. Anyway, thanks for your concern." Then she looked away, her shoulders sagging.

Patrick was quiet for a moment. Then he said, "I am a Christian, and there is this youth meeting that we normally hold every Friday evening. You may like to come and join us at the meeting this week. We are a group of sixteen to twenty-one-year-olds. It's always a very refreshing time."

Ihotu's face brightened up when she heard Patrick say that he was a Christian. She smiled at him and said, "Oh, really? I am a Christian too." Then she asked him, "Where does your meeting take place, and at what time?"

Patrick gave her the details, and she promised to meet up with them that same week. When Patrick had gone, Ihotu could hardly believe that there were other young Christians like herself in the College. If an Irish person tells you that he is a Christian, it usually means that he is a committed, Bible-believing Christian. Otherwise, when asked about his religion, he would probably say that he is a Catholic. For Patrick to voluntarily and boldly tell her that he was a Christian meant that he was more than likely serious about his faith. "At least I have something good to look forward to this week," Ihotu said to herself as she watched Patrick go.

On getting home that evening, Edache told her that he had sent some more money to her mum to help pay for her treatment. She was thankful to him for doing this. He made it look as if the money he sent to her mum was in compensation for not sponsoring her education anymore.

On hearing the news, she quickly rang Agada to find out when their mum would be able to start her treatment only to be disappointed when Agada told her that the money Edache sent was only a small fraction of what was needed to pay for it. He told her that the hospital was demanding at least half of the money to be paid upfront they could start any procedure on her. He also told her that they had approached so many friends and relatives, but none of them seemed to be willing or able to help any more. Ihotu knew at this point for certain that their only hope was God. She said, "Either God will heal mummy miraculously, or He will divinely provide the money for her treatment." She said these words to Agada to encourage him and to also reassure herself. With that, their conversation ended.

****

Finally, Friday evening came, and Ihotu showed up at the Christian Youth meeting. The atmosphere was electrifying. It was so good to see so many people about her age gathered together to worship God. It wasn't a huge crowd, but there were at least sixty people there. The interesting thing was that they all were from different ethnicity and were so friendly that she felt at home immediately. She had already spent one year in college and wondered why she never heard about this meeting before. The leader of the group, known as the pastor, was a young man by the name of Clem, who spoke with a British accent. He worked alongside his wife, Claire, who was a lovely petite lady with blonde hair. Her accent sounded very much Irish.

Clem was a slender man of average height and judging by the way he dressed; it seemed like he wasn't a person who paid too much attention to his physical appearance. Claire, on the other hand, was well-groomed and seemed like a person who would pay the minutest detail to how she looked. Both of them were probably in their early thirties. Ihotu later found out that Clem was an English-man who had come to Ireland for a project and had decided to settle there after he fell in love with Claire and they got married. At the end of the meeting, Patrick introduced Ihotu to them, and they were very warm and receptive. Ihotu immediately realised that she had fallen in love with the group and made up her mind there and then to become an active member.

Chapter 12

Joining the Christian Youth group was one of the best things that had happened to Ihotu in a long time. Now she found herself constantly looking forward to Fridays because of the meetings as they were always very refreshing for her. She often wondered if Clem and Claire were already aware of her pains and struggles as they always seemed to speak so directly into her life and circumstances. After about three weeks of being part of the group, Ihotu decided to make an appointment to have a one-to-one talk with them.

There was no doubt about it. Clem and Claire were the sweetest people Ihotu had ever met. Even though she had never seen Jesus Christ in physical form, Clem and Claire reminded her so much of the Jesus Christ she had read and heard about. They made her feel so confident, and Ihotu shared with them everything about her life and the current challenges with which she was confronted, especially regarding her college fees and her mother's ill health. She decided to be very open and truthful to them because she had heard it said that there were three kinds of people one must never lie to and these are your doctor, your lawyer, and your pastor. Obviously, if you lie to your doctor about what's wrong with you, he will give you the wrong prescription. Then, if you lie to your lawyer it will restrict his ability to defend you properly, and if you don't tell your pastor the truth, it will only make him give you the wrong counsel and his prayers for you, based on the story you made up, might actually work against you instead of for you.

As Ihotu talked to Clem and Claire, she felt so valued by the amount of attention they gave to her story and their patience with her. She didn't realise she was carrying so much on her mind until she found people such as these two who were willing to listen to her. She was pleasantly surprised, after speaking to them for so long and was finally finished; they asked her if there were any more things that she wanted to tell them. "These people are real saints. Beneath Clem's rough appearance is a very gentle and loving heart. And as for Claire, she is beautiful both inside and out." Ihotu reasoned as she continued to chat with them. As she talked, she realised the truth in the saying that 'a burden shared is a burden halved.'

"Ihotu," said Claire, "I can only imagine all that you have been through, and I know that it must have been really difficult for you. I want you to know that I can understand some of your pain as I have experienced similar challenges myself." Having said this to her, she took her hand in hers and squeezed it gently.

"Really?" said Ihotu, her face brightening up. She was eager to hear what challenges this beautiful, sweet and seemingly flawless lady, whose life looked like a bed of roses, might have gone through.

Claire went on to share how her own mother had also suffered from cancer several years before. She described how a point came when the doctors said they could no longer help her, and she was told that she just had a few more weeks to live. She asked to be taken home since the hospital could do no more to help her. At this point, she had lost so much weight that her skin had turned yellow, and her strength was virtually gone. Claire went on to say how her mum and dad were dedicated, faith-filled believers. On getting home, she said, her mum asked her dad to write out all the Bible verses that promised healing and long life, which he did. Then, she began reciting and declaring these verses several times every day, just like a person who is religiously adhering to a prescription given by a doctor. At first, it looked like nothing was happening, and sometimes she even feared that her mum was actually going to die. However, after a while, to everyone's amazement, her mum's health began to improve slowly. Rather than wasting away, her appetite returned, and she began to eat more food. Slowly but steadily, she began to regain her strength, and her skin colour began to return to normal, and that was how her mum got healed of what is so often called a terminal disease. As she finished her story, Claire declared, "I am happy to tell you that fifteen years on, mum is still alive."

Tears filled Ihotu's eyes as she asked, "You mean someone can actually be healed of cancer?"

"Yes, my dear," Claire replied. "With God, all things are possible."

"So is there hope for my mum to recover her health too?" Ihotu asked again.

"Of course, yes!" Clem chipped in. "The Bible shows us that God is not partial. He has no favourites. What He did for one, He can do for another. We are going to join our faith with yours and start praying earnestly for your mother. I suggest that you do for your mum the same thing Claire's dad did for her mum. Write out as many healing verses from the Bible as you can find and send them to her. Tell her to start confessing and declaring them every day." He smiled as he looked at her and said, "Every testimony has the power to reproduce itself." Then he continued. "And as for the challenge with your college fees, I perfectly understand what you must be going through because life was also very tough for me as a student when I was in college. However, I will spare you the details of my struggles as a student for another time," he said.

Claire was quiet for a while, trying to think of a possible solution. "Have you applied for a grant?" she asked.

Ihotu nodded. Then she explained, "You know how grants are means-tested. Based on my uncle's income, I did not qualify for it when I was entering college."

Clem saw that looking to God for help provided the best way forward. He spoke with assurance, "Let's continue to pray and see what God will do. Meanwhile, there are a few international students here who are members of our group, and they work in part-time jobs. We will talk to them and see if there are jobs on offer at any of their places of work."

Both Clem and Claire encouraged Ihotu to continue to be strong, knowing that God would be with her in whatever she was going through. They told her to remember always that this was a phase in her life which would pass after a while. After the long talk, they prayed with her and Ihotu left feeling so happy and light-hearted. Her faith had been rekindled, and she set out to do all that they had asked her to do.

She found about forty Bible verses about healing and long life, copied them and sent them to her mum. She shared with her mum the story of the miraculous healing of Claire's mother and encouraged her to do the same with the Bible verses she had sent her and to put her trust in God to heal her. It worked! Ahubi bought into the idea and began her journey of daily confessing and declaring the verses that Ihotu had sent to her.

As time went on, Ihotu's relationship with Clem and Claire got so close that she considered them more as a family than just the pastors of her youth group. They were so supportive. After the session that she had with them, either one or both of them would contact her almost every day to check on her welfare and to encourage her. She no longer felt alone facing her challenges. Through their help and that of Joan, one of the international students that they had spoken to, she managed to get a cleaning job in St. James' Hospital in Dublin. This job required her to work from 5.30am to 8.30am Mondays to Fridays, and for longer hours on Saturdays.

Ihotu was overwhelmed with joy when she heard that she had a job, but she got really scared when she was told the details of the working hours. "Starting work at half-past five in the morning! How on earth am I going to make it?" she said, voicing her fear to Claire when she was alone with her.

Claire tried to calm her. She told her that there were a lot of students like her who were doing similar jobs to finance themselves. Once again, Ihotu had so many questions racing through her mind. So, she asked Claire one thing after another, "So what time do they wake up? How do they transport themselves to work that early? Cleaning jobs require a lot of energy, so how can they cope with classes when they have to rush to college after work? Won't they be over-tired? What time would they have left for their studies?"

Claire tried again to keep her calm. "Ihotu, you are asking too many questions," she said. "I may not have the answers to all that you are asking, but what I can tell you is this, if other students are coping, then you should be able to cope as well. I want you to know that hard work does not kill; it just makes you stronger. Always remember that no matter how difficult things may be now, it is merely a phase that you are passing through.

Ihotu still looked unconvinced, so Claire helped her with some practical advice. "What you could do right now is to find out which bus comes from your area to James's Street and how long the journey takes. That will help you to work out what time you need to wake up to get yourself ready and be at the bus stop in time."

Ihotu took her advice and found that the journey from her house to the hospital would take about fifty minutes. This meant that she had to be up every morning by four o'clock at the latest. She then informed Edache and Ebere about her taking the job, and they had no objections.

Waking up at four in the morning, rushing to be at work by five-thirty, then rushing from work to be in college by nine, working in college until five in the evening and then trying to study and do assignments until ten at night wasn't an easy schedule for a girl under twenty years of age. She found the first week really tough, often dozing in class when it was getting near noon. As a result, she decided to start using a major part of her lunch-hour to have a nap, and she found that this helped to refresh her to some extent. The cleaning job was not as difficult as she had expected, and the three hours often passed quicker than she had envisaged. It was then that it dawned on her how much the house-chores that Ebere had assigned her had given her good training.

The part of the day that she found the most challenging was the evening period after her classes were over. She was usually exhausted by this time, so trying to study and do her assignments was a huge struggle. She normally just stayed behind in the library after lectures because, the few times she had gone home to try and get some rest before studying, Ebere had chores planned for her to do. This second year in college was becoming the most stressful year of Ihotu's life. She often said to herself that if she survived the year, she would not only complete her course, but she could survive anything that came her way in the future.

Ihotu just couldn't believe it the day she got her first wages! Two weeks after she started the job, a payslip was handed to her one day after work as her salary was paid directly into the bank. When she opened it, her eyes bulged with excitement when she saw that over three hundred euro had been paid into her bank account. She was so excited that she burst into singing and started dancing. Her colleagues, wondering what the cause of this sudden celebration was, asked her if she had just won the lottery. Laughing, she told them that her salary was her lottery. One of them, disappointed at her reply, said, "I can't believe that this meagre salary, which is hardly enough for anything, is making you celebrate like this." But Ihotu, still in her happy mood, replied, "If you had never owned a hundred euro in your whole life, then getting over three hundred euro would be a big thing for you."

On their way to college later that morning, Joan, who was not very comfortable with the manner that Ihotu had spoken so openly about her financial condition, asked her why she wasn't ashamed to tell everyone around her that she had never owned as much a hundred euro before now. Ihotu told her that the only way to help other people and to also ensure God's continued blessings is not to conceal your struggles and pains. "And, by the way," she said, turning to Joan, "aren't we all doing the same cleaning job? Surely, anyone who is well-off would not be doing this kind of work."

On arrival at college, Ihotu went straight to the office and filled out a direct debit form so that she could start paying her fees by agreed monthly instalments.

Chapter 13

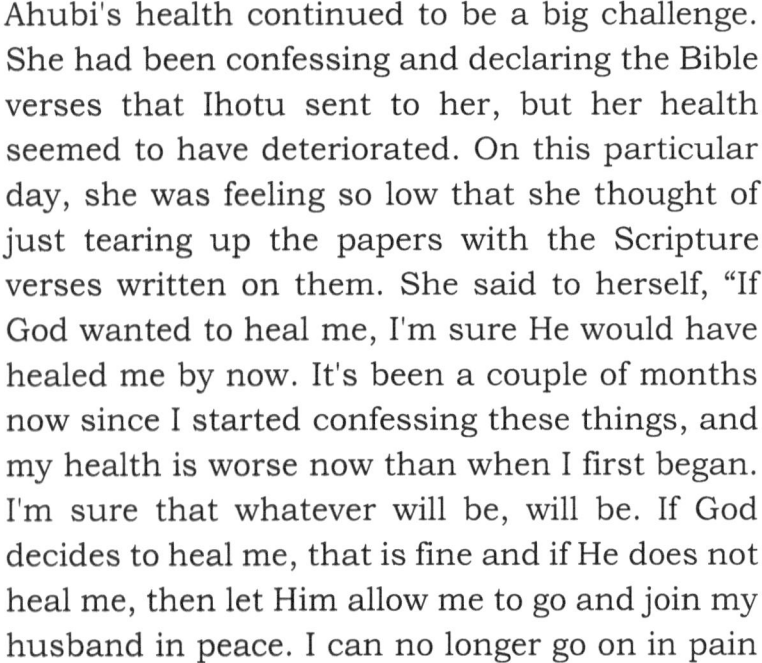

Ahubi's health continued to be a big challenge. She had been confessing and declaring the Bible verses that Ihotu sent to her, but her health seemed to have deteriorated. On this particular day, she was feeling so low that she thought of just tearing up the papers with the Scripture verses written on them. She said to herself, "If God wanted to heal me, I'm sure He would have healed me by now. It's been a couple of months now since I started confessing these things, and my health is worse now than when I first began. I'm sure that whatever will be, will be. If God decides to heal me, that is fine and if He does not heal me, then let Him allow me to go and join my husband in peace. I can no longer go on in pain like this. I am tired of everything!"

On second thought, she decided to discuss how she was feeling with Ihotu before proceeding with her intentions, so she asked Agada to ring Ihotu for her. When Ihotu answered, she was shocked at the words that were coming out of her mum's mouth and the tone of them. She had to cut in when her mum would not stop complaining and talking about everything in such a negative way.

"Mummy!" said Ihotu sharply, "I think you have said enough. Remember, when we were young, you used to tell us to keep quiet when we were talking too much? Today, with all due respect, mum, I am also going to tell you to be quiet. I understand how you must be feeling right now. You have become so overwhelmed by your pain and your problems that you want to throw in the towel, eh? Mum, have you forgotten all that God has done for us? Don't you remember that, if it had not been that God is on our side, our family would have been history by now? You want to go and join Dad, eh? What about us, Mum? You want to leave us as orphans, is that not so? Mum, just look at Precious and Agada who are there with you and reconsider what you want to do."

Having poured out her heart like that, Ihotu was filled with emotion and burst into tears.

After a long pause, her mother spoke. "Hmm.. my daughter, I'm sorry," she said, "It's just that this pain has become too much for me to bear. Look at me. I'm a mother who sees her children suffering but cannot offer them any help. I am suffering physically, I am in pain emotionally, and I am also financially handicapped. What kind of life is that? Why has life been so unfair to me?"

Ihotu, hearing the grief in her mother's voice, tried her best to reassure her, "Mum, life may have seemed unfair to us, but God has always been faithful. I believe we have gone through all that has happened for a purpose. You have helped us in every possible way that you could, and we are so grateful to God for you. We appreciate you, Mum. Don't worry, things will soon change for the better for all of us. You are certainly the best mum in the whole world."

Ahubi, at last, began to respond to what Ihotu was saying to her. "Hmm.... Thank you, *Ihotu kum*," she said. "What would my life have been like without you, and Agada and Precious as well? I guess I still have many reasons to live on in this world and to also give thanks to God."

To make sure her mother was continuing in this more positive way of reasoning, Ihotu went on speaking gently to her. "Yes, mum," she said, "You have plenty of good reasons to live, and you will have many more reasons to thank God shortly. That is why you cannot leave us now. Mum, you have to withdraw your previous statements by saying that you are not tired, that you are not going anywhere right now, that you will live and not die, and that you will live to see your children's children."

"Okay," said Ahubi, feeling remorse for the things she had been saying. She prayed, "God, please forgive me for every negative word that I have said today." Then she added, "I will not die now, but I will live to declare your goodness, and I will see my children's children to the third generation at least."

"Amen! That's better!" said Ihotu, laughing. "Mum, please don't tear up those Bible verses. Keep on confessing and declaring them boldly in faith and I am sure that what God did for my pastor's mum, He will also do for you. Remember that we are also backing you up in our prayers."

When Ihotu had finished talking to her mum, she decided to let Clem and Claire know about the situation as she was certain that they would have some good counsel to give her. Her guess was right as Clem told her that there was a need to back up their prayer with fasting.

"Can you do seven days fasting and prayer?" Clem asked Ihotu.

"Seven days? I could even do seventy days!" Ihotu replied, "Aren't I doing it to help my mum to get well?"

Clem smiled at her and said, "Claire and I will both be joining you for the seven days of fasting and prayer."

Ihotu was so grateful. She said to Clem, "Honestly, I don't know how to thank you both. You have been so good to me. I know that God in heaven, whom you serve and because of whom you are doing all these things for me, will definitely reward you. Thank you so much."

They agreed to begin fasting and praying from the following Monday, which was just two days ahead. Ihotu was happy that her college was on break and this gave her time to dedicate to the venture. Ihotu felt that Agada and Precious should join in the fasting and praying as well. After all, the larger the army, the stronger the force. She wasn't sure how long they could carry on in a day without food so she told them that they could break their fast at whatever time suited them. She encouraged them to miss at least one meal each day of those seven days and to make sure that they prayed during that time so that their fasting did not turn into a hunger strike.

A few weeks after they had completed their week of fasting and prayer, Ahubi told them that she had a dream in which she was in a very deep dungeon. Then someone came over to where she was, took her by hand, and brought her out. She said she noticed that when she woke up the following day, her appetite for food had returned and she had eaten better than she had done in months.

From that day, Ahubi noticed that her eating improved daily, and as she ate better, she also started feeling better, and her strength began to increase. Gradually, her pains also started to disappear, and she noticed that she was actually regaining her health! Her recovery was very gradual, but it was continuous. After another couple of months, she realised that she no longer felt any of the symptoms of leukaemia. It was only then that it dawned on her that God had fully healed her! To be sure that she was not just fantasising, she decided to go and see her doctor. On examination, after a series of tests were carried out on her, the results revealed that there were no traces of leukaemia in her body anymore.

Naturally, her joy knew no bounds, and she set out on a celebration spree. While she was discussing her plans with Ihotu over the phone, at one point they both became overwhelmed with emotion and began to weep for joy. Then Ahubi said, "A lot of people wonder whether miracles still happen? See me, *Ihotu kum.* My life is a living testimony that miracles are real, and they do still happen." She then went on to start pronouncing all kinds of blessings upon Ihotu, saying, "If it were not for you this miracle would never have happened."

To this, Ihotu humbly replied, "And I would also say that if it were not for my pastors, Clem and Claire, the miracle may not have happened at all." Then she added, "And I suppose Pastor Clem and Pastor Claire would attribute their strength and inspiration to some other person or persons. You see, mum, life goes around in circles. We are all meant to be there for one another."

"That's true, my daughter," Ahubi said, "but the only thing that saddens my heart at this moment, is that you can't be here for my super thanksgiving celebration."

Ihotu, even though feeling terrible about missing this joyful family celebration, tried to respond with some hope. "Don't worry, Mummy," she said, "Very soon, God, who healed you, will also make way for me to come home and see you. And, when I come, we will organise another thanksgiving party. Meanwhile, with the assistance of my pastors, we will also put together a special meeting in our church to celebrate the faithfulness of our God."

****

Following the miraculous healing of her mother, it seemed as if everything was beginning to turn around for good in Ihotu's life. By now, she was getting to the end of her third year in college, and due to her cleaning job, she had managed to support herself and also pay her college fees. She noticed that Ebere and Edache were now much nicer to her. She didn't know whether it was the testimony of her mum's healing or anything that had to do with her, but she noticed that both of them were getting much more serious about their Christian walk. A few days before, they had even declared a fast for the whole family, including Ene and Ehi. This had never happened in all the time since Ihotu had come to stay with them, in other words for more than ten years. Amazed at the change, Ihotu said to herself, "Anyway, I think this new development is a step in the right direction."

Although the cleaning job in the hospital had been a life-saver for Ihotu, as she was about to move into her final year in college, she began to pray that God would give her a better job. Her idea of a better job was one that would enable her to have practical experience in her field of study, and one where she would spend less time working but earn more money or at least about the same amount that she was earning in the cleaning job. This was because she really needed to give more time to her studies in her final year.

Chapter 14

One morning, as Ihotu and Joan were walking out of the hospital ward they had just cleaned, she said something that sounded funny and Joan, laughing at what she had said, shouted out her name, "Ihotu!"

"Ihotu?" Echoed an elderly black woman who was in a bed nearby.

Ihotu, realising that they were not supposed to make noise, began to apologise. "Sorry, ma! We're sorry if we disturbed you."

"Come over here to me, Ihotu," the woman said in a tone of voice that was almost like an order. When Ihotu went over to her, the woman asked: "Are you Idoma?"

Ihotu, surprised that anyone in Ireland could work out her ethnic origin from hearing her name, began to feel excited, "Yes ma," she replied.

"*Oiyim a*! (meaning my daughter)" the woman exclaimed, "Come, give me a hug."

Ihotu, though feeling awkward about doing this, responded to her request and hugged her. The woman introduced herself as Mrs. Aboje but explained that people usually called her, *'Enada'* (Ada's mum). She began to tell Ihotu the story of what had brought her to Ireland. She said she came to assist her daughter, Ada, who had had a baby about three months earlier, to nurse her baby. She went on to say that she then went down with the flu and received treatment at Ada's home from the family doctor. When she wasn't getting better, the doctor referred her to the hospital, and after a series of tests, it was discovered that she also had a kidney infection. She said she had been in the hospital for over a week at this stage. And so, on and on went Enada, talking to Ihotu as if she had known her all her life.

"Ihotu, we're running late," Joan, who had been waiting all this time, called out.

Ihotu didn't want to leave just yet, and so she answered, "Just one more minute, Joan."

"Where are you off to, my daughter?" Enada asked her.

"We're on our way to school ma," Ihotu replied.

"Is there a school in this hospital?" Enada asked her again.

"No, ma. We come here every morning to work before we go to school," Ihotu replied.

Enada realising that she was delaying Ihotu, said, "In that case, don't let me delay you any longer, my daughter. But please come back to see me when you get a chance." As Ihotu walked away, Enada said out loud to herself, "So there are Idoma people here in this country?"

The next day was Saturday, so, after work Ihotu came back to see Enada again. She brought her some drinks and some fruit. Enada was delighted to see her and introduced her to her daughter, Ada, who was with her when Ihotu arrived. Enada was such a cheerful and chatty woman, telling them so many funny stories. She was supposed to be the patient, yet she was the most cheerful person in the ward. In the course of the conversation and inquiries, Ihotu discovered, amazingly, that she was from the same village as her dad and had even known him.

Enada was amazed to discover that she knew Ihotu's family. "You mean Mr. Ameh was your father?" she said. "He was such a nice, hardworking man with great prospects. Ah, death is so cruel!"

Then Ada spoke up. She saw that her mother's reminiscing could upset Ihotu. "Mummy, that's enough," she said. Then she turned apologetically to Ihotu and explained, "My mum could talk from now until tomorrow without getting tired." Turning back to her mother, she said, "And by the way, before I forget, Mum, Oche told me while we were talking on the phone yesterday that he will be coming in to see you today." Then she added, "I thought he would have been here by now."

Enada smiled at Ada and nodded her head, "He told me the same thing when he rang me yesterday. Maybe his flight has been delayed." she said. However, she had hardly finished speaking when Oche walked into the ward.

Enada's face beamed as she welcomed him, "You are really the son of your father. We were just talking about you." she said, with real warmth in her voice.

"I thought you were coming this morning," remarked Ada.

"Yes, I wanted to, but I had to change my flight because I needed to be at a meeting this morning that was taking place at the church which one of my friends attends," Oche explained.

His mother, hearing this, cut across the conversation. "My son and church! As if all the church meetings you have been attending in Nigeria are not enough, you come over to London for a brief professional conference, and you still squeeze church meetings into your time there."

Oche looked lovingly at his mother, his face brightening despite her apparent criticism, "Mum, you should be happy for me that I have chosen to live my life in God's way. That is what has helped me come this far in life," he said graciously.

His mother's voice softened. She looked up at him and reaffirmed her support for his Christian stance. "Oche, I am really happy for you. When I look at the responsibilities you carry and how you are able to achieve all that you have done, I know that you are not serving your God in vain."

Then Ada, realising that Ihotu was being left out in the conversation, decided to introduce her to her brother. "Ihotu, please pardon our rudeness. Meet my kid brother, Oche. Oche, this is Ihotu, a friend that mum met here in the hospital."

"Who is a kid?" Oche said as he stood up to shake hands with Ihotu. As his eyes met hers, there seemed to be an immediate kind of chemistry between them. As soon as she touched him, he felt a strange sort of connection with her. "What a beauty! This girl is so cute," he thought as they exchanged pleasantries. Ihotu, on the other hand, also felt a strong attraction to him too, and as she chatted to him, she was even thinking, "Wow! Cool! And to think that he loves God just like I do." In fact, they both silently wondered, "Could this be love at first sight?"

Enada then began a narrative about Oche to Ihotu. She said, "Oche is the youngest of my three children. He studied Mechanical Engineering in the United Kingdom and started to work there after his graduation. That was until his father pleaded with him to come back home and take over his construction company in Abuja, as he was about to retire. Oche initially did not like the idea but three years on, he seems to have adjusted very well to his new situation and has even taken the company to even greater success. He has come over to London for two weeks for a professional conference, and that is why he can come to see me here in Dublin."

"Is it three years already?" Ada asked.

"Yes, time flies so quickly when you're busy," Oche replied.

Then Enada also went on to tell Oche how she met Ihotu. Then she added, "And could you also believe that I knew her late father very well?"

Oche laughed when he heard this. "Isn't it a small world that we are in," he remarked.

In the course of their conversation, Oche discovered Ihotu's need for a better job, and he volunteered to speak to a friend of his who ran an accounting firm to see if he could be of any help in assisting Ihotu to get a part-time job in the accounting sector. He really liked her, and he was going to take advantage of this opportunity to keep in touch with her. He was true to his word, and a couple of weeks later, Ihotu got a part-time job with an accounting firm. She only had to work for three days a week but earned slightly more than what she had been getting in her cleaning job. Talk about receiving answers to prayers! Her prayers for a change of job were answered in full.

As time went on, Oche and Ihotu became close friends. Normally, he would visit the United Kingdom about two or three times a year for business or conferences, and he came over to

Dublin to see his sister and friends on some of those visits. However, since he met Ihotu, he found himself looking for the slightest opportunity to travel as he repeatedly wanted to see her again. As a result, he was in Dublin every other month.

****

Her college studies had been progressing very well, and Ihotu's final exams were now very close. One day, just before the start of her exams, Jane and Abbey approached her, saying they had something very important to discuss with her. They found a quiet place to talk, but Ihotu became both shocked and confused when the two girls knelt in front of her and began to plead for her forgiveness.

Not understanding what was happening, Ihotu tried to stop the girls from doing what they were doing. "You guys are embarrassing me, please get up off your knees so we can talk," Ihotu said to them, feeling completely bewildered.

They got up off their knees and sat down. A long silence ensued, which was only broken when Ihotu asked, "What do I need to forgive you guys for?"

There was a long pause. Then after a while, Abbey spoke up. "Ihotu, both of us have treated you very badly. We lied against you and betrayed your trust." Then she paused again, and Jane continued the talk, "Remember those emails to Steve and Kunle Ade? Actually, we made them all up," said Jane, looking very contrite.

Ihotu felt like screaming when she heard what Jane had just said. "You did what?" she exclaimed but quickly calmed herself down.

"We're really sorry, Ihotu. We don't know what came over us," Abbey said, and she went on to give the full details of what they had done. When she finished, there was another silence for a while. Then Ihotu asked, "Those emails were written in May, but you sent them to my aunty in August. Why was that?"

"Actually, we delayed sending them when we learnt of your mum's illness," Jane replied.

"And it must have been you guys that told my aunty that I had sent money to my family in Nigeria as well," Ihotu said as the rest of what had been written in the emails came back to her.

Jane and Abbey nodded. Ihotu could see from their expressions that they were totally ashamed of themselves.

"Hmm....." Ihotu sighed as she began to recollect all that had happened and the trouble she had been through. "If only you guys knew what trouble these actions of yours caused me. Do you know that my uncle stopped paying my college fees after what you did? Are you aware that I had to do a cleaning job for two years just to make sure I remained in college? I confided in you when my mum was sick, and my siblings were starving, and I had to send them the only fifty euro I had managed to save in a whole year." She could hardly talk any longer as she burst into tears. After sobbing for a while, she looked up at Jane and resumed talking, "Jane, I gave you my student account password because I wanted to help you. So why then did you turn on me and use it against me?"

Jane took one of her hands, and Abbey held the other as both of them wept with her. Then Jane spoke. "Ihotu, please forgive us. We did those things without thinking about the possible consequences, but now we see that no matter what we did on you, you have remained ahead of us. We're really sorry, Ihotu. Please do forgive us."

"To prove how sorry we are, we don't even mind going to your aunty and telling her the truth," said Abbey. "We don't want to leave this college with guilt on our conscience. That is why we have decided to admit what we did and ask for your forgiveness. Will you please forgive us, Ihotu."

"It's alright," said Ihotu. "I never held anything against you guys in the first place. It's just that your admission today has brought up a lot of painful memories which I never wanted to remember. It's okay; I forgive you." She said, her smile returning.

"Really?" said Jane and Abbey almost simultaneously as both of them hugged and thanked her.

Ihotu could see there had been a huge transformation in the two girls, but what they said next amazed her even further. "We heard that there is a Christian youth meeting that you always go to. We would love to go with you to the next one if that's alright," said Abbey.

"Yeah, that's right. Both of us would really love to go with you," Jane added.

The girls really showed their change of heart when they said to Ihotu that they wanted to put right what they had done that had upset her family. Jane said, "Right now, we need to go and tell your aunty and uncle the real truth about those emails."

"Can we come home with you this evening and talk to them, or should we send an email to your aunty?" Abbey asked.

Ihotu shook her head. She was pleased with the girls' offer, but she still hurt from how Edache and Ebere had treated her. Looking at the girls, she said, "Honestly, it doesn't really bother me any longer whether you tell them the truth or not. They chose to believe what they wanted about me irrespective of the life they saw me living. Whatever you choose to do is fine by me, but I don't plan to be home until about nine-thirty this evening as I want to do some more study in the library."

However, despite Ihotu's response, Abbey still decided to send an email to Ebere. In her email, she told her the truth that she and Jane were responsible for the emails that purportedly were sent from Ihotu to Steve and Kunle.

Abbey's explanation did not really surprise Ebere as she had guessed all along that there was something fishy about those emails. She, however, had taken and used the information because of her resentment for Ihotu as she saw them as good evidence to use against her.

As Ebere looked over Jane's email again, she suddenly felt very guilty for the first time about how badly she had treated Ihotu. She realised that, despite everything she had done to frustrate and destroy Ihotu, she still had not succeeded. Many thoughts went through her mind. "How will I make things right now? How will Edache react if I show him the new email from Abbey? Should I just ignore the email and carry on as if I hadn't seen it?"

She tried to ignore what Abbey said in her email for a couple of days, but her conscience would not let her rest. Eventually, she decided to tell Edache. By now she had decided to make a new commitment and take her Christian walk much more seriously and so she didn't want anything to hold her back anymore. To her surprise, when she showed the email to Edache, rather than blame her for what happened, he took his share of the blame for acting so rashly and jumping to conclusions about Ihotu, and he regretted that he had stopped paying her college fees. After deep reflection, he said to Ebere that both of them would have to apologise to Ihotu and do it as soon as possible. Ebere was very much in agreement with this.

So, early the following morning, they invited Ihotu to their room. Edache began the conversation by getting straight to the point. He said, "Ihotu, we called you here because of another email that your aunty received from your friend Abbey. We now know the truth, and we want to tell you that we have not been the best of guardians to you. In fact, we have treated you very badly. Please forgive us." He paused for a little while and then continued, "I know that African culture does not encourage an adult, especially a man to apologise to someone much younger than he but you have so challenged us to reach a higher standard than we had before that I just have to apologise to you. I am really sorry for the way I treated you, Ihotu, I really am."

Ebere, feeling too guilty to even look at her, said, "And me too, Ihotu, I'm very sorry for how I have mistreated you. Please find it in your heart to forgive me."

Seeing how remorseful both Edache and Ebere were, Ihotu spoke reassuringly to them, "It's okay, Uncle, Aunty. If you hadn't taken me from my village and brought me to Ireland, would I be where I am today? I owe both of you a lot of gratitude for all that you have done for me." Then remembering the hurt caused by their distrust, she added, "The thing that surprised me all the time is how you chose to believe the worst instead of the best about me."

Edache looked straight at her. Then he said, "We are much older than you, and we should have known better. However, we are human, and we make mistakes sometimes. We got it wrong, and that is why we are asking for your forgiveness."

"It's okay," Ihotu responded, looking at both of them with a smile.

"So, have you forgiven us?" Edache asked.

"Yes, I have, Uncle! And you too, Aunty! Ihotu answered. Then she said, "I actually forgave both of you long before today. I forgave you because I saw that God has a way of turning what we call misfortunes into blessings, and He has been doing this in my life all the time."

"Yes, we can see that," Edache responded. "Thank you for forgiving us."

"Thanks, Ihotu," Ebere joined in as they both hugged her.

Epilogue

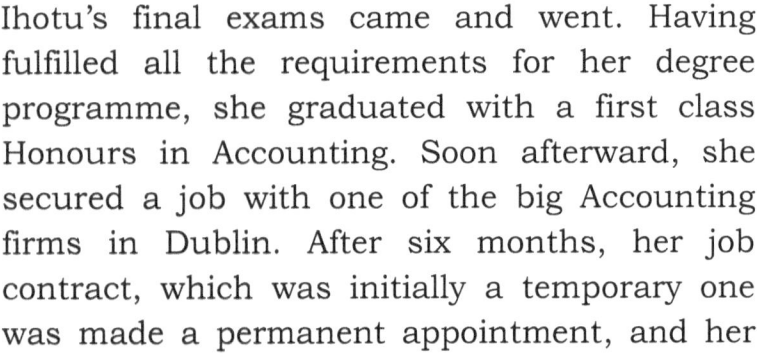

Ihotu's final exams came and went. Having fulfilled all the requirements for her degree programme, she graduated with a first class Honours in Accounting. Soon afterward, she secured a job with one of the big Accounting firms in Dublin. After six months, her job contract, which was initially a temporary one was made a permanent appointment, and her company enrolled her for professional exams that would qualify her as a Chartered Accountant.

When Oche came over to Dublin for her graduation ceremony, he asked Ihotu to marry him, and she happily accepted. When they told Edache and Ebere about their decision to get married, they were really pleased. Edache, joking, teased her, "Can you see what your hospital cleaning job has landed you? This tall, handsome, and successful guy!"

They all laughed, and Ihotu in replying to her uncle said, "Uncle, when I said that God has a way of turning misfortunes into blessings, you think I was kidding? Now, you can see real evidence of it."

180

"In fact, this evidence is undeniable," Ebere added, and they all laughed the more.

"You are all talking as if it was only Ihotu who gained," said Oche. "What about me? Where would I have met such a beautiful, hardworking and intelligent girl, if it weren't for that hospital job?"

They all agreed in unison that everything really works out for good for people who love God.

****

After she had settled into her job, Ihotu was able to travel home to see her mum, her brother and her sister, a real treat after about thirteen years of separation! During her visit, Oche brought his people to meet her people, and a wedding date was fixed. She then returned to Ireland for the completion of her professional exams and, thankfully, she passed every one of them at the first attempt. She planned to return to Nigeria for the wedding, which was to be held a few months later and afterward to settle there with Oche.

With the memory of the story of her life and how she had managed to survive all the difficulties, Ihotu suddenly felt quite confident that the storm currently raging outside was not going to last forever.

Acknowledgements

My most profound appreciation goes to my family, who have supported and encouraged me immensely. I want to thank my daughters, Ochanya, Olijeh, and Eyum (Jnr) for their insightful contributions, especially regarding the young characters in this book, and Grace for her cooperation by giving me space.

Deaconess Yemisi Ojo, Barrister Francis Obiabo and Ochanya Ocheola-Oki, thank you so much for taking the time to proof-read this book and for helping me see my characters from your point of view.

Gordon Harper, your contributions to this book are invaluable. Thanks a million for the long hours that you spent editing it.

And to many others whose names I cannot all mention here; may God bless each of you real good for all your support.

CONTACT

For more information about Eyum or to order any of her books (digital or hard copy), please visit:

www.amazon.com
https://okadabooks.com
www.mypainyourgainministries.com

You can also connect with her by:

Email: info@mypainyourgainministries.com

Facebook: @MyPainYourGainM

Instagram: @MyPainYourGainM

YouTube: My Pain Your Gain Ministries

ALSO, BY EYUM EJIGA

In this inspirational book, Eyum tells the story of the shock, pains, and trauma that she went through following the birth of her daughter, Grace, and the steps that she took to receive comfort.

"He Gave Me Comfort" is a captivating story of a mother. It's a book that you will not want to put down until you finish reading it! This book will not only bring you comfort but will it restore your hope no matter the circumstances in which you find yourself and inspire you to reach even greater heights. It is a must-read!

SOME REVIEWS OF 'HE GAVE ME COMFORT'

"This work is very well written. It is like an emotional roller-coaster. As you read it, you will laugh, cry, meditate & pray. In all of these, you appreciate the awesomeness, mercy & faithfulness of our God. The author's faith & story are very moving & encouraging."
Pastor Tunde Adebayo-Oke
Dublin Ireland.

"He Gave Me Comfort" is an inspirational & amazing book that touched and moved me when I read it. This is a book that must be read by every human being on the face of the earth, as reading it will inspire, challenge, comfort and help you focus on God and trust Him for the best even when you find yourself in difficult and unexpected circumstances.
Dr Elizabeth Omole
London, United Kingdom

I picked up this book with the intention to gloss over some aspects of the work with the aim of facing it later. From that first moment, I could not put it down. I could see life-changing lessons poured into the pages of this book in pure emotion and utmost candour. I was also spurred by the richness of the material. This book will not only strengthen you to deal with any immediate challenge you may have right now, but it will also equip you for the future.
Rev. Simeon O. Afolabi
Port Harcourt, Nigeria.

This is a very inspiring book that has blessed me richly. It teaches a Christian's response to life's perceived challenges while portraying an ALL-knowing God who never makes mistakes. The author exposes these facts in an easy to read way using her own experience and those of others. Once you start reading, you can't stop until it is done. It will be a valuable addition to any library as this is a book you will want to pull out again and again when those perceived challenges rear their ugly heads as they sometimes do. I want to assure the author that her reason for writing this book has been accomplished with me because this book ministered to me in a deeply personal way.

Judith I
Ontario, Canada

I recommend that everyone read this book and get encouraged and comforted through every situation they might be going through. The book seemed like fairy tale or something you only see in movies, but I had to keep reminding myself that I know the characters involved. You cannot understand until you read it and once you start, you cannot stop. We give all the glory to God.

Omobola Adejayan
Dublin, Ireland

This book has been a tremendous blessing and eye opener to me, I can't wait to read it over again.

Lucky Musa
Dublin, Ireland

This book is a must-read! It has blessed the people I have been privileged to give and me. I must say it is an emotional story, but it will challenge your spiritual life as God opens your eyes to new revelations in the book.

Joyce Ukponu
Dublin, Ireland

This book really blessed me. It gave me a different perspective on life. Life is a gift, so appreciate God every day. Thank you, Sister Eyum, for sharing your life experiences with me.

Amen Amusan
Minnesota, United States of America

This is a must-read book, not just for reading sake but a book that will make you to discover your weaknesses and strength, if you've not been through certain challenges, you will never discover your God-given potential. A Book that will transform your life and know that all things work together for good "To those who Love God".

Yinka Sanni
Dublin, Ireland

A great book to read! A good book to read when you're going through something you can't make any sense of. This book will let you know what God says about the uncertainty of life.

D. Johnson
Dublin, Ireland

About the Author

Eyum Ejiga is an accountant and entrepreneur. She has chosen to write to inspire, inform, and impact as well as entertain her audience. She had contributed articles to various magazines and newspapers in the past and currently blogs, her blog theme known as 'MY PAIN, YOUR GAIN.'

Although, writing comes naturally to Eyum; she never saw herself as a writer until she decided to pen the painful experience she went through following the birth of her last child who was born with a severe disability. She recorded her experience in a book entitled 'He Gave Me Comfort,' which was her first book. The wide-spread acceptance of this book and the numerous positive reviews it received made Eyum venture more into the world of writing. This is her second book and her first work of fiction.

Amongst other qualifications, Eyum holds a B.SC (HONS) in Computer Science from University of Benin, Nigeria; B.SC (HONS) in Applied Accounting from Oxford Brookes University, United Kingdom; and a PG Certificate in Digital Marketing from National College of Ireland.

She is blessed with four gorgeous daughters, Ochanya, Olijeh, Eyum (Jnr) and Grace.

www.ingramcontent.com/pod-product-compliance
Lightning Source LLC
Chambersburg PA
CBHW031111260626
47172CB00001B/320